Below the spaceship [...] alien city, a vast asse[...] very high and thick wall surrounded the city, and this brought curiosity from the star-travelers.

"A wall is usually meant to keep something inside or else outside. Being around a city, I should say that it is to keep something out."

"The something must be a colossus to require a wall as large as that one."

"Not necessarily a colossus. The wall may require special height to keep out a type of creature whose natural facilities enable it to jump very high—or the menace may carry means of climbing."

But even as the Zoromes spoke, the monstrous creatures that threatened this peaceful alien settlement were approaching, unseen. And they presented a danger so incredible that the men of Zor could never have guessed its nature!

This is the fourth in Ace Books' exciting series of
PROFESSOR JAMESON SPACE ADVENTURES

For information about the earlier books
in this great saga, see page 158.

TWIN WORLDS

by

NEIL R. JONES

ACE BOOKS, INC.
1120 Avenue of the Americas
New York, N.Y. 10036

TWIN WORLDS

Printed in U.S.A.

Contents

Contents

TWIN WORLDS

PROLOGUE

THE PROFESSOR'S EARLIER LIFE and biography is more or less irrelevant to our story. Where we become interested in him and directly concerned with his career is in the October of his life. He dreamed of preserving his dead body against the inevitable law of nature much as had the Egyptians, yet his dream crept deeper into the realms of eternity than those of his predecessors.

Nearing the end of his life, he built a radium-propelled rocket to find an orbit around the Earth, where in its cosmic coffin his body would remain forever unchanged, free from bacteria and other Earthly effects. He left full instructions for his nephew to act upon subsequent to his death. Silent and glistening, ready for its strange career, the rocket rested against the eight tracks of its slanting tube, waiting. During this wait, the professor foresaw and forestalled the menace of meteors. Automatic radium repulsion rays, their source kept continually rejuvenated by a process of transformed sunlight, answered the problem.

The vigil came to an end; the professor died. He passed away on a December morning not long before a late risen sun burst forth to flood the countryside with the rare novelty of December sunshine. His nephew was stunned by the secret instructions left him, yet acted upon them nevertheless. There was the lonesome trek at midnight through the snow-mantled cemetery: the pilfering of the grave vault, the emplacement of the body in the rocket, the tripping of the radium release, the hurried run for shelter, and Douglas Jameson remained the only comprehending witness to the rocket's plunge into space. The incendiary firing of the ejector building with its clustered laboratories followed as an aftermath, the roaring, devouring flames consuming all traces of the professor's secret. For many long years, the secret was kept, but one day Douglas Jameson, still working in the interests of his deceased uncle, told the world. It was generally classified as a hoax, despite the empty grave vault in the Grenville cemetery, until the discovery by Clement

7

years later. With his telescope, he discovered and charted the course of the Jameson satellite on its orbit sixty-five thousand miles distant from the Earth.

Years passed. Decades slowly rolled into centuries. Centuries passed by thousands—then ten thousands. History grew multifold. Mankind, life on Earth, rose and fell, finally disappearing off the face of the aging planet. Still the professor in his rocket satellite circled the Earth. More than forty million years fled by, the rocket circling Earth constantly like a tiny moon. Professor Jameson had accomplished his great ambition. Yet how true it is that men plan without taking into consideration the caprices of fate, that unmoved destiny which rules the courses of worlds apart.

It was one of fate's caprices which brought a party of space wanderers, machine men from a distant corner of the universe, into the shadow of the dying world, a planet lifeless and untenanted, a pathetic semblance of past glory. They found the lonely rocket satellite revolving about the Earth on its endless orbit.

The machine men of Zor had achieved immortality by removal of their brains from organic bodies of flesh and blood to machines which knew replacement and repair rather than death. A cubed body, four metal legs, six metal tentacles and a metal, cone-shaped head enclosing the vital brain presented a weird but practical aspect. Conveniently encircling the metal head were shuttered eyes, working much on the same principle as television, a single eye in the apex of the coned head permitting upward vision. They communicated by means of mental telepathy.

No greater surprise can be imagined than that of Professor Jameson when he came to his senses and found himself a machine man. The Zoromes had transferred the brain from his perfectly preserved corpse to one of their machines and had recalled it to life. He found himself a machine man, a convert to the ranks of those scientific wanderers of the cosmos who journeyed from one planetary system to another, exploring the myriad wonders of an unending argosy.

Professor Jameson was given the numeric title 21MM392, and he became a seasoned mariner of the cosmos. He visited strange worlds and met with even stranger adventures. He found weird, unearthly forms of life living in environments where life would not have been suspected, and he encountered unusual forms of intelligence among the creatures the machine men discovered on their travels.

8

I

SWIFT AND SILENT, like a wandering meteor, the spaceship of the Zoromes flitted into the swelling brilliance of what from a distance had been a glowing point against a jet background of vast, illimitable space, only a star among myriads of stars, but now, on closer proximity, a gigantic sun, a perpetual furnace of the cosmos.

Thirty-nine machine men gazed in eager anticipation as the various planets were picked out and classified. Delicate instruments supplemented the mechanical eyesight of the Zoromes.

"There are four planets," Professor Jameson summarized after careful examinations had been made. "Two of them on the opposite side of the sun, one at right angles to our approach and another we will soon pass."

The worlds on the other side of the sun, two in number, glowed as small, fixed orbs of light, duller and less scintillating than the fiery stars in the vastness beyond. One planet directly at opposition with the spaceship's approach, appeared like a tiny full moon, while a companion world, further removed from the sun, appeared through the telescopes as a gibbous orb. The world at right angles was visible as a quarter sphere without the aid of magnifying instruments.

The world they were soon to pass lay directly ahead of them and was not visible since the side they were approaching was the night side.

"One thing seems certain," was 744U-21's opinion. "The world which we are soon to reach will be possessed of no atmosphere. Had it air, we should be able to see it even though we are coming toward its dark side. Suffusion of sunlight through the atmosphere often produces a circle of hazy light."

20R-654 turned the course of the cosmic traveler to one side as they came within a quarter million miles of the nearest planet. Like a great arched silver light, the horned crescent of the visible world loomed large. Closely, the machine men examined what they could see of its surface.

9

"There is no air," said 12W-62. "It is unlikely that the planet supports life."

"Its surface is a vast, frozen desert."

"The world rotates."

More of the huge planet became visible as the spaceship passed to one side. One quarter of the entire surface now lay open to the examination of the machine men. They discovered from afar only a dead, barren and apparently uninhabited span of desolation.

"21MM392!"

The professor turned from his position at a telescope as 41C-98's thought wave struck him, a thought wave tremulous with rising excitement. The professor believed that 41C-98 had possibly picked out some startling detail of the world they were passing, a detail which had so far escaped the examination of the others. To his surprise, he found that the machine man was not even looking at the world they were passing. He was staring off in another direction without the aid of a telescope. His mind vibrated to discovery.

"There are five worlds, 21MM392, not four!" he exclaimed.

"Is there one further out in space that we missed?" the professor queried.

"No! There is a world between the two we saw on the other side of the solar body! The nearer of the two eclipsed the one we failed to see!"

"A remarkable coincidence," the professor observed.

All the machine men now stared across space at a new planet seemingly not far removed from the nearer of the two worlds they had previously seen.

"The central one of the three planets must be very large," said 119M-5, "for from this distance it appears nearly as large as the other one which is much closer."

Glasses were leveled in the direction of the newly discovered world. The planet behind them, growing from gibbous to full, was nearly forgotten.

"That world is not far removed from the other, 119M-5," 29G-75 stated from his position at a telescope. "They are very close."

"Does it possess an orbit of its own around the sun?" queried 744U-21.

For a short time, the machine men observed the new world carefully.

"It seems to revolve about the other world."

"A moon, a very large moon," 6W-438 observed.

"Nearly as large as the planet itself."

"I believe you will find on further examination that the two bodies revolve about each other on a common orbit about the sun," the professor stated. "They are undoubtedly twin worlds. One is as much a moon to its companion as it is vice versa.

"They are third in line from the sun. There is but one outer world beyond their orbit."

The professor now took the glass. Carefully, he estimated the distance between the two worlds as not much more than a hundred thousand miles, while their respective diameters he figured were five thousand miles and five thousand, five hundred miles.

"One of them is inhabited, I believe!" 744U-21 exclaimed. "I can see what appears to be a city on the smaller world!"

"Are there many of them?"

"It is rather hard to tell."

The spaceship came closer to the objects of the machine men's scrutiny. At the professor's suggestion, the ship was driven between the twin worlds, giving the machine men a closer view of both planets. From a distance of fifty thousand miles, they examined both worlds.

"I am sure of the city I saw on the smaller world," said 744U-21, "yet now that I look at the same spot where it should be, according to the speed of rotation, I can find nothing but a vast expanse of water."

"It is strange," 6W-438 agreed. "The same thing happened with me in the case of an island I was viewing."

"Both worlds possess an abundant atmosphere, yet the smaller one seems to be all water."

"Not like a hydrosphere?" 9ZQ-435 interposed.

"This cannot be entirely a world of water," observed 56L-426, "for we have already seen land surfaces upon it."

"Yet where is the large island on which I saw the city?" queried 744U-21.

"There must have been some mistake in the estimation of distances and rotation," the professor offered.

"Wait!" cried 29G-75 in rising spirits. "A huge continent on the larger world is coming into view!"

From the watery wastes of the smaller world, the instruments of the Zoromes were now leveled at its slightly larger contemporary. Slowly, a great continent, dark and rugged in its shadows, bright and dazzling where the sun struck, swung into sight. The space ship clung to a restricted area

11

between the two worlds as the machine men took their observations and gathered data. Fully forty degrees of the planet's equator were visible from where the machine men had halted their spaceship, both worlds appearing as quarter-moons. Because of atmospheric aberration, poor seeing was prevalent upon the horizons.

If the machine men were excited merely by the appearances of several inhabited islands on the smaller world, what they saw on this larger planet now dwarfed into insignificance what they had seen upon its twin sphere. Large cities showed plainly, yet the spaceship lay too far distant for the machine men to pick out the inhabitants.

"If the original builders inhabit those cities, they must be possessed of an advanced intelligence," the professor stated.

"Shall we land?" asked 20R-654.

A short consulation decided the issue. They circled both worlds several times, examining all sections before choosing a spot upon which to land.

The decision was finally reached to land upon the smaller world, on one of the many islands which dotted the continuous ocean.

A peculiarity of the smaller, water-bound world attracted them. On the isolated islands were small clusters of strange buildings not unlike those on the other world. A careful examination of the other planet had disclosed no spaceships, although in their observations, strange vehicles had been found for use on the sea, on the land and in the air. There appeared to be no spaceships, yet the scattered dwellings on the smaller world bore a distinct architectural relationship to those on the larger sphere.

Strangest of all was the solution to 744U-21's enigma. With one of the telescopes, he had sighted an island on which was built a small city. Later, on closer approach of the spaceship between the two spheres, he fully believed that what he had previously glimpsed was but a mirage. For where the island and its buildings had previously been, there only tossed a restless expanse of unbroken water. 27E-24 had suggested the coincidence of a subterranean settling of the planet at that particular place and time. But such coincidences are to be proved before being accepted.

The coincidence was disproved. The disappearance of the island was caused by the heavy, sweeping tides oveer the lower land surfaces as the planet swung toward its neighboring world. These tides were very high, swelling to meet the attraction of the great globe rolling through space a hundred thousand miles distant. Only the higher portions of the various islands escaped this daily inundation.

"But how could anyone live in the city we saw buried beneath the waves?" queried 12W-62.

There are several explanations which might serve," 41C-98 offered. "The inhabitants may be amphibious, possessing the adaptation for living in submersion for a passing period of time. Then, too, the buildings we saw engulfed by the rising tides may be on abandoned islands that have sunk beneath the flow tide level."

The machine men picked out one of the islands on that side of the planet away from the other world. They had a half day in which to explore before that hemisphere swung about to face the companion world. Tides would then flood to the high water mark. Preliminary investigation had proved that this island was among those not entirely submerged at high tide. It was long, rising high at one end and sloping gradually into the sea at the other end. Fully half the island or more lay revealed at high tide. Buildings clustered and dotted the perpetually dry section of the island, while at the opposite end of the island only one building kept solitary vigil. Of all the buildings on the island, however, it was by far the largest. It was built much like a castle, yet without the turrets, towers and other straggling features characteristic of the castles the professor had known. This great building was built massive and compact.

It was at this lower end of the island that the machine men of Zor first decided to land. Coming down, they skimmed but a few miles above the more thickly settled portion of the island's highland. At the glasses, machine men uttered mental exclamations.

"There is life of some sort existent down there! Creatures move about among the buildings!"

"They possess vehicles of a sort, too!"

"What can that great wheel be for?" 744U-21 mused. "It is larger than the buildings around it."

Professor Jameson directed his glass in the direction of a gigantic wheel mounted upright among the squat dwellings below them. At first, it appeared to be resting on the ground, yet closer inspection revealed the fact that it hung suspended on standards, its circumference well clear of the ground. Small buildings lay clustered below it, while various apparatus surrounded the spoked giant with its narrow rim.

13

"They must be industrialists who worship the wheel as a means of utilizing power," 41C-98 ventured. "It may be an idol of theirs."

"Industrialists are generally of a different psychological composite," the professor stated. "That big wheel serves a purpose, perhaps of pumping something from the ground."

"Certainly not water," 12W-62 reflected. "They have all of that they want."

"Unless they pump fresh water," 119M-5 added.

"There seem to be no walls or dikes erected, so it cannot be used to keep a part of the island dry during the period of submersion."

"This part of the island is not submerged," 119M-5 reminded 41C-98.

"We shall find out more about that wheel after we have investigated the lone castle to see what kind of life, if any, it harbors," the professor promised.

The spaceship of Zor landed not far from the massive pile which possessed but very few apertures, and these appeared to be set with either transparent or translucent barriers of some substance yet indeterminable. Also, these windows were all located far above the ground level of the castle which latter was built of dark gray rock, somber and discolored through the endless action of the tides. To all outward appearances, the place was untenanted. Discussing the huge, silent structure and its possible hidden mysteries, the machine men approached it, as with metal feet they trod over damp mossy ground where here and there the last tide had left a puddle of water.

"Who are you things of metal who think and talk silently among yourselves?"

Crisp and clear came this mental utterance, halting the advance of the machine men as they stopped in momentary stupefaction. Someone other than themselves had spoken, presumably from the confines of the dark stone building. It was tenanted, evidently, and the machine men were being watched closely.

"Speak to me, that I may understand," came the telepathic voice. "My mental faculties are not up to your standard. Where are you from? Are you robots from Dlasitap under remote control?"

"We are machine men from a far-off world of another planetary system," 744U-21 replied. "Our brains are organic, such as yours is probably, too. Our bodies and appendages are mechanical."

14

"We come with friendly intentions," Professor Jameson added. "Will you not come out? We stopped here out of curiosity."

"Space travelers!" exclaimed the hidden speaker in unconcealed respect and admiration. "You have completely mastered the art of space travel, then! How wonderful!"

There came a pause. The machine men waited patiently for the owner of the voice to appear. Finally, the telepathic conversation was resumed. The speaker, however, still remained invisible.

"I am coming to you. It is not easy to leave this place after it is sealed against submersion. We have already opened and closed it for our daily air supply. Do you understand me clearly? I can understand you quite easily, now that your thoughts are directed to me."

"Your building is waterproof?" queried 6W-438.

"Yes, it is quite necessary if one is to remain here. You may have guessed as much before you landed."

As the machine men watched, they saw a portion of wall rise from within an indentation of the building, twenty feet or more below the ground level. A long ramp was thrust slowly out and downward, as if operated mechanically. Upon this slow moving ramp stood the castle's tenant whom they had heard and now saw.

The machine men of Zor stared curiously at the diminutive figure on the ramp, the outer end of which softly touched the ground and came to rest. The intelligent creature was little more than half as high as the machine men and possessed a small, globular body mounted on four appendages. An elongated head rose from the body, a single eye, large and round, staring inquisitively at the machine men from the center of the long head. The machine men believed the creature to be possessed of no upper appendages, and they wondered at this until they saw one of the lower limbs drawn up suddenly to shield the single eye from sun glare as the castle's inhabitant walked out on the ramp from the depth of shadow cast by the huge pile. The four appendages served a double purpose and could be used for handling objects, possessed as they were of four digits each.

They could discern no means of respiration or the means of induction for food sustenance, but as the creature turned a bit one of their previous observations taken for granted was quickly exploded. There were two of the large eyes. They were situated exactly opposite each other, an eye on each side of the head. Another important fea-

15

ture became apparent. There was no front or back to the creature; it progressed equally as well in either of two directions.

"What do you live upon?" the professor asked. "How do you breathe?"

"I eat—that is how I live," came the reply to the im-impulsive question. "Oh—you probably do not see my mouth, and that is why you are left wondering."

Reaching the end of the ramp and stepping off upon the sodden ground, the strange creature bent his body, or rather, bent two of his legs at their joints, so that the machine men could view the top of his head. An aperture opened and closed several times at the apex of his head.

"There is my mouth," he exclaimed. "I inhale and exhale the necessary atmosphere through these."

He designated ventricles scarcely noticeable at the junction of his head and body. There were several of these.

"I am Kamunioleten."

From the top of his head came the vocal utterance of the name he could not pronounce mentally. The only thought impression the machine men gained of his name were several strange symbols of which they possessed no knowledge and had no key to the relationship of sound thereto.

II

"WHY DO YOU LIVE on this lower portion of the island which is daily submerged by the tides?" Professor Jameson asked. "Why not live on the higher ground?"

"I live here because I have been made to live here," Kamunioleten replied. "I am an exile, an exiled Administrator of Dlasitap, the world which causes the great tides here on Selimemigre."

"Then you have spaceships!" 744U-21 exclaimed.

"No—not spaceships like yours," Kamunioleten corrected. "The vehicles in which we cross space are not under their own motive power. They are projectiles. They are hurled across space from one world to another—though as yet we have never reached any of the other planets. The other worlds are much too far and our efforts too crude compared with yours, and until we can construct spaceships which travel under their own power and can be handled skillfully, we must forego such ambitions."

"How are your projectiles hurled off into space from

one world to the other?" 6W-438 queried. "Do you use cannons?"

"No. We employ the expedient of centrifugal force coupled with a diminution of gravity at the point where one world faces the other," was the explanation. "During your examination of Dlasitap, did you see any of the large wheels which tower as large as many of the buildings?"

"We came not that close to Dlasitap, but we saw a large wheel on the higher end of this island and wondered at it," 41C-98 replied.

"What supplies your motive power for the revolution of the wheel?" the professor inquired.

"We heat water in a huge, enclosed container," Kamunioleten explained. "The water turns to hot vapor which expands, and we utilize this expansion as our power."

"Steam!" Professor Jameson exclaimed. "You use steam power!"

"Crude, yet nevertheless ingenious," 744U-21 remarked. "Your wheels must certainly be strong or else they would fly apart from the rapid speed at which they must be driven."

"Not so rapid as you might possibly think," said their informant, "though it is true that such catastrophes have occurred before now, especially in the earlier days of travel between the twin worlds. That, however, is but one of the many hazards."

"We can gather then," said the professor, "that the far reaching gravitational power of one world nullifies to a marked degree the gravity of the other world at the position of highest tide and makes for less required inertia of centrifugal force."

"I could have explained it to you no better myself," Kamunioleten commented admiringly.

"What keeps your ships, or cosmic projectiles, from crashing?" 744U-21 asked.

"The wheel is slowly accelerated to a speed which will throw the projectile just beyond the attraction of the planet from which it is being thrown and into the pull of the other world. For deceleration, we possess atmospheric contrivances which remain folded into the rear of our projectiles while they are being shot into space. When they reach the atmosphere of the opposite world, the contrivances are gradually released so that the deceleration does not occur too quickly."

Kamunioleten went into a description of stabilizer fins,

17

and then he told them of a broad disc of metal, which, using the projectile as an axis, spread fanwise about it in ever increasing diameter, acting as an air brake. Last of all, he told of light, metal parachutes folded into the projectiles and released as soon as the air brakes had taken effect. Always aimed at an oceanic body, the projectile released the parachute just before striking the water, allowing the projectile to dive deeply into the fluid, losing its momentum, and then coming to the top.

"The parachute contrivances are recovered from the surface of the water, for they are built of segments of hollow metal. We always dive into the sea. A careless aim, or ill timing, may mean a descent on land, a catastrophe which always spells death and destruction."

"And so, in your floating projectile, you wait until a boat comes, or else you drift in to land," 12W-62 suggested.

"That is the easiest part of all," Kamunioleten told the machine men. "The projectiles possess motive power to drive them through the water."

"Steam is again employed, I suppose," 29G-75 ventured.

"It also heats our projectiles during the great coldness which comes between worlds," Kamunioleten stated. "Insulation and triple partitions help a lot, too."

"It must be a great adventure," Professor Jameson mused. "Do these ships of yours cross space very often?"

"Not so often," Kamunioleten told them. "There are too many hazards, as you can well appreciate. Wheels have broken under the terrific strain to which they are subjected, projectiles have been released prematurely, or accidentally, flying off into space on an endless journey or smashing into the ground, either of which is fatal. Then, overspeed or else insufficient acceleration have caused tragedy through miscalculation. Projectiles have missed their mark, or not having been given enough push have fallen back upon the planet they were to have left. In the latter case, especially with projectiles leaving this world, passengers have been saved through the good fortune of the projectile's having landed in deep water."

"It is a wonder that anyone dares to travel that way," marveled 19K-59.

"That is but the beginning," continued Kamunioleten, dwelling pessimistically upon his morbid subject. "Projectiles improperly aimed often fall upon land surfaces of the opposite world, more likely if traveling from Selimemigre to Dlasitap, which is the mother world, the home world, the original birthplace of our race. This means a smash; a smash means death and junk. There are also hazards in space, in the air and on the sea. If no part of the projectile is ruptured in its flight through the atmosphere, thus letting heat and air leak out into space, is not struck by a chance meteor, its deceleration contrivances may become jammed and unmanageable.

"Projectiles that have survived the trip across space and hit the water have been known to sink, too, through too great a water pressure from its dive into the sea. This fault is largely due to insufficient deceleration or else a failure of the parachute to become unattached before the projectile hits the water, or the projectile may not hit the water straight through clumsy or belated release of the parachute."

As Kamunioleten enumerated the various hazards connected with this primitive mode of cosmic travel, the machine men saw that he was exaggerating the possibilities of mishap to the projectiles. They also saw that the cause for this lay in a melancholy outlook, a brooding fatalism which held sway over the mind of this intelligent creature. He was depressed, and his weighted spirit sought expression and release in this gloomy retrospect of space travel.

A comment by 6W-438 probed the cause of this dissatisfaction which had evidenced itself in Kamunioleten's pessimistic attitude.

"You spoke of being an exile."

"Yes. I am the deposed Grand Administrator of Dlasitap, kept here as a pawn in the hands of my evil successors. They are tricky and cunning: enough so to have put me out of control and to keep me exiled here. The twin worlds have rotated about the sun more than seven times since I first came here."

"Why do they keep you exiled instead of killing you?" asked 744U-21. "The latter way would seem much easier for them."

"They dare not kill me, for then the nations of Dlasitap would rise up against them, and against each other, and their false story might be proved untrue in the event of such a grave situation. Proof of my continued existence is their safety."

"But why do they keep you here at this lower end of the island?"

"They intend to keep me out of contact with the colonists of this world. They fear that someone may believe my

19

story and that its credence will spread to Dlasitap and prove their undoing."

"Can you not journey to the higher end of the island during low tide?" Professor Jameson inquired. "Or are you under guard here?"

"I am the master here," Kamunioleten replied. "I have three Vosquenteb servants here, a lower race which we found to be the original inhabitants of Selimemigre. Otherwise, I am alone. As for journeying to the island's higher end during low tide, it is much too far to be made on foot before the next high tide. My enemies have planned well."

"How were you overthrown?" 744U-21 queried. "You spoke of trickery."

"It might be well for me to first explain our governmental system on Dlasitap," said Kamunioleten, seating himself upon the ramp, his four legs spread equidistant like spokes of a wheel. "I have hopes that you may be able to help me, if you will. This idea occurred to me rather quickly right after you landed, probably because I am always looking to the day when a discovery will take place on Dlasitap, when the undercurrent of evil in the present rule of government will be uncovered, as it seems to me that sooner or later it must be. Then, I feel, I shall be brought out of exile by the public masses."

"What happened?" 6W-438 probed the mind of the exiled Administrator for the crux of the problem.

"There are seven nations on Dlasitap," Kamunioleten explained, "and each nation sends a group of officers to the Grand Assembly, the governing body of Dlasitap. Long ago, it was found that nations could not rule themselves individually and still retain amicable relations. Of this governing body, there is an administrator for each nation, standing at the head of each nation's group of officials in the Assembly. Chosen by popular vote of the Grand Assembly, one of the Administrators is elected Grand Administrator."

"And you were the Grand Administrator, I take it," Professor Jameson interjected.

"I was," Kamunioleten related. "But there were lesser members of the Assembly who sought my power and the power of the other Administrators of whom there were six besides myself. Their aims, though appearing to the general public as satisfactory, were inwardly selfish, and they were encouraged by monopolists who secretly backed them. But the people were satisfied with us, and as our terms are

20

indefinitely long, these malcontents, under the leadership of Bemencanla, awaited a chance to strike.

"We Administrators were not suspecting any such active, violent move as was made by Bemencanla and his followers. There comes the annual trip to Selimemigre, when at least five of the Administrators must make a tour of the colonies here to be assured that they are being properly governed and that the natives, the Vosquentebs, are being fairly treated. As you have gathered, I am rather reluctant about traveling in the stellar projectiles which seem so hazardous and unsafe, and as there were five others of the Administrators either eager for the trip to Selimemigre as a well earned vacation, or else willing and indifferent, I did not go. Neither did Owmitelverol, who is old and not well.

"The five Administrators choose one of the smaller projectiles with a crew of three besides themselves, and the projectile was placed on one of the power wheels. On the day that they left, it was a shocking story that reached me, and it left me both horrified and bewildered, for at that time I was unable to piece together the schemings and perfidy of Bemencanla all at once. The bombshell struck and left me stunned until after I had been whisked away to this island on Selimemigre.

"The projectile with its eight occupants, five of them Administrators of the Grand Assembly, had been released at the wrong time, or I should say, at the wrong position of the wheel, being shot into space at a tangent direction from that of Selimemigre. Our scientists say that such ill-aimed projectiles will keep on through space forever, unless they fall into the attraction of another celestial body. They lived, no doubt, until their food or air gave out."

Kamunioleten paused in moody contemplation. 744U-21 urged him on with his story.

"And in some way you were accused of having planned the accident?"

"Exactly. It seemed that, unknown to me, a group of my countrymen were in charge of the wheel and apparatus which sent the ill-fated projectile off upon its endless journey, and this was strange, for it was in a country other than my own where the projectile left Dlasitap. Afterward, none of the operators of the wheel could be found. In fact, for some time here in exile I believed they would be found and my innocence established. But they were never found, and I gradually came to understand that this was but more of Bemencanla's scheming. He had somehow

21

bribed these countrymen of mine to attend the wheel and send the projectile off in an undestined direction. Their escape and disappearance was planned, and I would not be too sure but what Bemencanla saw that death overtook them, so that they might not live to tell."

"What motive could be fastened upon you as the instigator of the deed?" the professor asked.

"Bemancanla possessed a ready weapon. Others of the Administrators had opposed a measure of mine recently, and although it was not overly important, this event magnified its purport. In my exile, I am rarely visited, and even then Bemencanla, who is now elected Grand Administrator, sees that only his own minions are allowed to visit me. I hear but little of what goes on upon Dlasitap. All I ever see of my own world is before and after high tide when it is distinguishable as a great globe lying upon the horizon, for as it commences to rise in the sky, the waters pour over my castle, and Dlasitap disappears as a blur in the green depth above me."

"And what of this Owmitelverol?" Professor Jameson asked. "What did this surviving Administrator think of the affair? Did he condemn you, too?"

"I do not know," Kamunioleten confessed. "I was removed here to Selimemigre too swiftly. I was quite sick on this first trip of mine across space, for despite the devices employed to lessen the centrifugal force on our bodies while our projectile is being revolved, I felt myself flattened and thought that I would not survive the ordeal. I lost my senses momentarily as most of us do on the start of such trips."

"It will not be long before the great tides sweep over your castle," Professor Jameson reminded Kamunioleten. "Dlasitap is rising upon the horizon."

It was true. Shining pale and gibbous in the sunlight, the twin world was slowly rising into the sky. Its ascension heralded the rising tides.

"Come into the castle—all of you," invited Kamunioleten. "There is plenty of room indeed for you all. I have but three of the Vosquentebs here. You will find them a stupid lot, but they are nevertheless faithful."

"We shall be glad to come in and talk more with you, Kamunioleten, for your story interests us," said 744U-21, "but as for your fears of our survival against the rising tides, let me put you at rest. We are as much at home in the water as in the atmosphere, though it is true that move-

22

ment in the water is slower, and currents of water are stronger upon us than are currents of air."

"You are marvelous creatures," was Kamunioleten's admiring observation, "and I am truly thankful that of all systems in this vast universe you should pick this one to investigate at this particular time."

"It is more of a coincidence that we should have picked this one spot on Selimemigre on which to land," 6W-438 made mention, "though it is obvious that once in this system of worlds our attention would immediately be attracted by the twin worlds."

The machine men filed into the castle over the long ramp, leaving six of the Zoromes to man the spaceship. 20R-654 had orders to float upon the surface of the ocean in the castle's vicinity until the tide should have gone down.

"Come to the top of the castle," offered the exile, as the last of the machine men stepped off the ramp. "From the topmost roof we shall see Dlasitap rise and pull the waters of Selimemigre so high that we shall no longer be able to see Dlasitap."

Kamunioleten led the way to a broad, spiraled stairway which funneled its way to the topmost ramparts. And what a queer stairway the machine men found it to be. The professor had never seen its like before. All the stairways he had seen on the planet Earth had been a rising succession of steps. On Zor and its sister worlds, there had been no stairways. Sloping ways led from one level to another, much like the ramp on which they had walked into the castle, while the higher levels were always reached by mechanical means. This stairway, however, represented a seemingly haphazard, upward succession of blocks. Kamunioleten hopped up them nimbly, while the machine men picked their way carefully, lest they stumble along this unfamiliar path. It was a strange stairway, but a stairway to fit the mobile appendages of one like Kamunioleten to perfection.

On the way to the roof where Kamunioleten wished them to watch the inundation of the castle, they passed three or four levels. On one of these near the spiral stairway, they suddenly caught sight of one of the Vosquentabs. It was a slender creature standing, like Kamunioleten, on four legs, yet its body was long and slender, and its head was not so high nor as prominent a feature. The eyes were situated lower on the head, and, instead of being placed opposite each other; they were closer together. The mouth,

23

though situated above the eyes, was not on top of the head, as in the case of Dlasitap's inhabitants. The professor discovered in the Vosquentebs only a remote resemblance to their conquerors from the other world. Somewhere, in the remote past ages, there must have been some connection between the two species, for their body structures were not greatly dissimilar. An unintelligible talk was carried on between Kamunioleten and the Vosquenteb, the machine men sensing instructions given by the exile to the others.

III

IN THE EXCHANGE of enunciated syllables, the machine men observed that the Vosquenteb referred to the race of creatures from Dlasitap as Emites. Their syllables, coordinated with the accompanying thought impressions, referred to Kamunioleten in terms similar to "great Emite," and in the minds of the Vosquentebs, as they later discovered, all of Kamunioleten's species were classified as Emites.

The machine men, led by Kamunioleten, passed on upward to a flat roof of thin, stone slabs carefully cemented. Yet, when queried by the professor, Kamunioleten disproved the assumed supposition that the stonework was waterproof. The waterproofing was done on the inside, rather an intermediary layer of building material between the inner and outer walls.

When Zoromes and their host reached the square platform of the highest roof, they fairly crowded it. Dlasitap, now well above the horizon, climbed slowly toward its zenith, or, more correctly, the zenith of its rise represented by the island's position on the surface of Selimemigre.

Kamunioleten pointed afar. "Look," he said. "The tides are coming."

And the tides were coming. Undulating waves rushed forward in the distance as upon a beach, yet they did not recede, the water level creeping ever nearer until the waves washed the base of the castle, swirling curiously about the spaceship of the Zoromes. More waves washed lazily about the castle, accompanied by a perceptible rise of the water level, as if subterranean aqueducts were quietly pouring their contents into the swelling ocean. As Dlasitap crept higher in the sky, the water came ever higher as if to meet it, which in itself was an actual truth.

"The highest tides are those with the sun behind Dlasitap," said Kamunioleten, "yet this tide will inundate the castle completely, for it is always so."

The water level rose rapidly now, the spaceship awash and bobbing about like a cork. The boundary where the gradually receding beach met the lapping waves hurried away in the direction of the distant highlands. Like a sinking ship, the castle floundered deeper in water until the illusion would seem almost true were it not for the stabilizing sight of a hazy horizon of substantial ground. The water crept to the edge of the roof on which the Emite and the machine men stood. Kamunioleten looked longingly upon his home world rising in the sky above the far horizon formed by distant hills, but he roused himself suddenly.

"We must go below at once!" he urged them. "The castle will soon be completely submerged!"

On all sides, the rising ocean lapped the castle walls, while a little to one side towered the spaceship of Zor, floating and bobbing upon the watery expanse. The mellow glow of Dlasitap's gibbous face yielded to one of more intense brightness as it rose higher in the sky. The machine men and Kamunioleten hurried into the little superstructure and down into the castle, two of the Vosquentebs closing the watertight door behind them. This was scarcely accomplished when a gentle ripple of water crept over the roof they had just quitted.

The professor, 744U-21 and Kamunioleten returned to the interior of the superstructure at the latter's suggestion and gazed through the thick, transparent windows. Waves swirled above the castle, making the bright, gibbous face of Dlasitap seem indistinct and distorted, the twin world apparently dancing crazily about and changing its shape in quivering, shimmering movements. Blue sky yielded to gray translucence as Dlasitap became vague through the watery expanse overhead, gray deepening to dull green which grew steadily darker. The roving hemisphere of night was commencing to creep over that section of Selimemigre.

Kamunioleten gave what was equivalent to a sigh as the rising orb of Dlasitap grew indistinguishable through the surging, overwhelming flood. He led the way down into the castle once more, and behind him walked the two machine men. 744U-21 questioned the Emite concerning the lost ship of the five Administrators and its crew of three.

"And did you ever know what became of the lost projectile?"

"It is still traveling off into space at its initial rate of speed which it possessed when it left the attraction of Dlasitap, doubtless," was Kamunioleten's sad rejoinder. "Besides being aimed wrong, the projectile was given excess speed; otherwise it would have slowed to nearly zero beyond the attraction of Dlasitap. Eight bodies stiff and stark in death—yet maybe they are better off than I am; who knows? Yes, even as over seven years ago, the projectile and its passengers are still traveling through the endless space, headed for an endless destination."

"Seven years?" 744U-21 echoed in query.

"Seven years," and here Kamunioleten paused in thought. "Seven years and one hundred and six days, to be exact— that is, seven of Dlasitap's years. You see, I have little else to do here in exile other than keeping track of such things, yet they brew morbid thoughts."

"What difference is there in Dlasitap's year from that of Selimemigre's?" Professor Jameson inquired. "It must take both of the twin worlds the same length of time to circumnavigate their common orbit about the sun."

"The difference is this," the Emite explained. "Selimemigre turns faster upon its axis than does Dlasitap. Dlasitap's year of one hundred and seventy-eight days has fewer days than has the year of the twin world. The day of Dlasitap is divided into eighteen whegs. It takes Selimemigre but eleven and five-sevenths whegs to make a full turn upon its axis; that is, estimated roughly. Of course, Dlasitap being the original home of our race, all calculations are based upon its unit of time."

"Was there any estimate obtained concerning the speed of this lost projectile?" 744U-21 inquired curiously.

"Our astronomers lost sight of it long ago through their strongest glasses, and several years have passed since it dwindled from sight, but, from what word has been given me in my exile, I have learned that a nearly exact estimate of its speed was obtained. The ill-aimed projectile left Dlasitap's gravitational attraction traveling at the rate of one thousand, three hundred and eighty-four borgs per wheg. There is no reason to believe that during the ensuing years this rate of speed has altered."

"None indeed," 744U-21 agreed.

"Unless a meteor impact should deflect the direction of flight, or change the speed," the professor interpolated.

"Yes, that possibility does exist," said Kamunioleten, though it seems remote."

A long time the Emite and machine men remained in discussion, Kamunioleten sitting down at a broad table through weariness of physical structure from which the machine men were immune. They talked of the lost projectile in space, of space flight between the twin worlds, of Bemencanla's perfidious treachery and of how best the machine men might reinstate Kamunioleten, for they had developed a genuine sympathy for the unfortunate exile.

Among other things, they came to conceive of Kamunioleten's references to time and measurements. Reduced to Earthly terms, Professor Jameson learned that a borg measured 7.193 feet and some few inches; also that the day of Dlasitap divided into whegs equaled sixteen hours and forty-eight minutes, not measured to the exact second.

"The projectile traveled about two thousand, twenty-one of my Earth miles per hour," was the professor's final summation to 744U-21.

When the tides had receded, Kamunioleten once more opened the way leading out upon the roof. He and the machine men walked over the damp rock, where little pools of shallow water dotted the concavities. Both the sun and Dlasitap had gone to rest, the latter recently set, a luminous patch of sky marking its descent into the horizon. Kamunioleten pointed among the twinkling stars to a glimmering point of light near the zenith; then he designated another star barely distinguishable to the naked eye, not far from the first.

"Astronomers of Dlasitap could give you more accurate information of a nature better simplified than my own," he told them, "but exactly forty-seven and six-eighths of the distance from that brightest star on a straight line to that faint one is the direction taken by the lost projectile. With the naked eye alone, I am told, it is the best way of computation."

The machine men were fully agreed upon helping Kamunioleten in his misfortunes, and they were anxious to see the nearby world of Dlasitap and its civilization. 744U-21 was for an immediate embarkation with Kamunioleten in the spaceship of the Zoromes to Dlasitap, proclaiming the duplicity of Bemencanla and his minions with the return of Kamunioleten to his proper status once more.

At this vision conjured in the forceful mind of the machine man, a glow of enlivened hope shone in the eyes of the Emite, yet his countenance began to be troubled.

"No, that would not be the right way, at least not the

27

best way," he averred. "I not only want to win back my power, but the faith of the people as well. Too firmly has my supposed treachery been intrenched in the minds of the peoples of Dlasitap. I may thank Bemencanla for that. I would know what Owmitelverol thinks, if he lives, as well as my most loyal supporters, not to mention the general populace. I can return better prepared, if I know the situation that exists on Dlasitap and how the people take to the rule of Bemencanla and his officials."

"And you want us first of all to go to Dlasitap and find out these things?" Professor Jameson anticipated for the Emite.

"Yes. Then you can return and tell me, after which we shall know best what to do."

They returned to the ground level. Once more the tides were receding, and the spaceship of the Zoromes rested on dry ground close to the castle. One of the Vosquentebs had opened a way to the west ground surrounding the castle, and the machine men were walking about examining various forms of sea life left by the receding waters, many of these aquatic species struggling valiantly to return to the green depths which had so magically rolled away upon the horizon, a horizon which Professor Jameson had observed as less distant than upon worlds the size of, or larger than, his Earth.

Near the ground level, the professor and 744U-21 found two of the Vosquentebs bailing water from a lower portion of the castle, bringing it up to the ground level in large buckets and pouring it outside where it trickled into rivulets and pools.

"What are they doing?" the professor asked.

"There is a leak below the ground level of the castle," Kamunioleten explained. "Of late, it has grown worse. Within the past few days, we have found it necessary to empty the lower keep of water. I spoke about this leak the last time I was visited by the supply ship which sails here on the high tide every eleventh day. It will come again, soon, and on it I expect suitable repairs for this growing leak."

The machine men returned to the spaceship and held a consultation. It was decided that Kamunioleten's advice concerning a more complete knowledge of the present situation on Dlasitap should be adopted as a plan of action. Professor Jameson thought it well for a few of the machine men to stay with Kamunioleten until the rest returned, if for no better reason than to keep him company, as well as to aid the Vosquentebs in keeping the lower regions of the castle dry after high tide. Kamunioleten was delighted to learn of this turn of affairs, especially when he learned that the professor and seven more of the machine men were going to stay at the castle with him while 744U-21 and the rest were crossing space to Dlasitap.

Once more the waters rolled up over the castle, burying it in the green, translucent depths where finny denizens of the deep ogled curiously at the moving forms in the castle seen dimly through stalwart, transparent windows. At low tide, the spaceship of Zor rose into the sky and headed for Dlasitap, leaving behind on the island the professor and seven metal companions. of these, there were 6W-438, one of the professor's closest associates on his cosmic adventures, and 5ZQ-35, once on Triped on the planet of the double sun and known as Glrg, both of them from the old expedition. Then there were 777Y-46, 19K-59, 8L-404, 65G-849 and 948D-21.

Days passed uneventfully. There always came the inevitable tide on its restless journeying, regularly enveloping the castle as Dlasitap towered above the horizon and went through its various phases in relation to its twin world and the sun. The sun rose and set, and when the sun lay high in the sky with Dlasitap, the tides were higher, as was evidenced by the increased pressure. No better gauge of the pressure was needed than the leak in the cellar of the castle. As Dlasitap reached its zenith, and the waters buried the castle at its deepest, there spurted from the ruptured masonry a strong parobola of water.

As Kamunioletan had said, the leak was steadily growing worse. The machine men helped the Vosquentebs bail the water out of the lower level of the castle to keep the ground level dry. In fact, had it not been for the machine men, the Vosquentebs could never have bailed out all the water before the next tide rose. But as the professor pointed out, the worst Kamunioleten might expect from the leak would be a flooding of the ground level during the high tide, and this might easily be disposed of by opening the sealed doorways and letting it run out at low tide. In that case, it would be necessary to retire to one of the upper floors. Kamunioleten received this reassurance philosophically, yet with an uneasy bit of pessimism.

"So it might be if the leak in the wall grew no worse, yet daily it allows the entrance of more and more water. It is well that I soon expect the supply ship with the necessary repairs."

Professor Jameson mentioned the probabilities of numerous eclipses due to the close position of the twin worlds, to which Kamunioleten made affirmative reply, asserting that the eclipses, though common, were unusually impressive because of the sun being generally hidden entirely from sight, only its strong rays visible in a halo of atmosphere surrounding the opposite world. Eclipses were rarely seen from the castle, he told the machine men, because they usually occurred when Dlasitap was hidden from sight by the towering waters.

The supply ship which the Emite had been expecting came one day. As those upon it were more or less in the employ of Bemencanla, Kamunioleten thought it better that the machine men remain hidden and see, in the minds of those who came, as much as it was possible to ascertain. So from their vantage points the machine men saw the great, flat, steam-driven boat settled slowly with the tide and finally come to rest on the island not far from the castle.

The boat was manned with Vosquentebs as well as Emites. Many of the latter left the boat and came to the castle, Kamunioleten having already let down the long ramp to the main entrance. The Emites entered, and the machine men sensed much conversation between them and Kamunioleten. Later, both Emites and Vosquentebs were busy bearing large boxes and other supplies from the drydocked ship to the castle. Then came the high tide once more, rising slowly at first from out of the distance, then gaining proportions quite rapidly until the supply ship floated far above the sunken castle.

During the interim, the Emites from the boat repaired the break in the cellar of the castle, assuring Kamunioleten that he had nothing more to fear from leakage. On the next low tide they regained their ship, to lie in wait for the next high tide. When the waters lowered again, with Dlasitap slowly sinking below the distant skyline of water, the boat was gone, nor could it be seen anywhere in the distance.

All during the stay of the visiting Emites and Vosquentebs, the eight Zoromes had remained in hiding. Now they came forth once more, finding Kamunioleten eager to discover what, if anything, the machine men with their keen mental faculties had learned from the visitors. Professor

Jameson summed up the consensus of the machine men in a declaration of warning:

"Somehow or other, they do not mean well by you, Kamunioleten. As you yourself have said, Bemencanla would have you killed if he dared, yet for matters of state he must keep you in exile. From our position where we could not observe them, it was a bit more difficult for us to probe their thoughts, especially as they were not directed at us as are your thoughts. Also, their mental designs were a bit garbled and mixed to our susceptibilities. A malign regard is borne you, and these Emites aboard the supply ship are a party to it."

"Which is little more than to be expected," Kamunioleten added, "for Bemencanla would see that no friends or sympathizers of mine were put in contact with me."

"Bemencanla fears you, then, in spite of your seemingly impotent position," said 6W-438. "This fear of his is your chief danger, for, if it were possible, he would have you done away with."

IV

THE NEXT HIGH TIDE allayed any fears of Kamunioleten that the old leak would cause further bother, for the Vosquentebs reported that no water had leaked into the castle. Meanwhile, the machine men were expecting the return of the spaceship from Dlasitap. Regardless of the fact that 744U-21 had set no specific time for his return, the professor felt that by this time those aboard the spaceship must have discovered what information they believed would be valuable to the exile on Selimemigre.

Yet each lowering tide showed no return of the spaceship. The machine men commenced to suggest various possibilities.

"Do you imagine that some mishap could have overtaken the spaceship?" 948D-21 offered.

To this there was no direct reply, and the fearful speculations continued. Yet it was 6W-438 who spread a bit of optimism upon the subject.

"They may have found something which calls for a longer stay than they had previously anticipated."

"Those aboard the spaceship may have forgotten the exact position of this island," was 19K-59's hopeful contribution to the general conjecture.

"We can only wait and be patient," Professor Jameson

stated. "I recollect that I had a seven hundred year wait once in a wrecked spaceship."

Kamunioleten stared aghast at the professor's matter-of-fact revelation, an episode in the system of the double suns.

"While I waited that long at the bottom of a broad ocean pit," 6W-438 added.

"You had the company of fourteen companions, while I was alone," the professor reminisced.

Kamunioleten was curious and intensely interested in the adventures of the machine men, and while they awaited the return of the spaceship they related to the Emite many wonderful things, what they had seen and events which they considered outstanding among their cosmic travels. Kamunioleten listened in awe and rapt attention.

During the time Kamunioleten found it necessary to sleep, the eight machine men were left to their own devices. The three Vosquentebs they found to be true representatives of a humble, dull-witted species, and they afforded the Zoromes little diversity in the performance of their duties. Several times the machine men went on a small tours of the surrounding island both at low tide and at high tide. The Emite was greatly astonished to see them moving about under water from his vantage point inside the castle."

It was during one night at high tide that a startling occurrence broke the monotony of ceaseless waiting. Kamunioleten lay asleep, and the Vosquentebs were either asleep or otherwise occupied in the upper reaches of the castle. On all sides and above, the water lay deep and unfathomable to the eyesight. Silence had replaced the washing and swishing sounds made by the water rising about the castle, for now the isolated pile lay buried in the green depths of the sea. The eight machine men were gathered on a middle level of the castle in preoccupation and idle conjecture as to what at that moment might be happening to those who had left in the spaceship. A gurgling, washing noise of water came to their mechanical senses of hearing.

"What?" exclaimed 8L-404. "Is the tide commencing to drop so soon?"

"It doesn't seem early enough for it," said 777Y-46.

"Nor would I say that it was," 6W-438 observed, peering through a transparent square of the castle's outer wall into the black water. "But it is night outside, and the varying periods and heights of the tide in relation to the positions of Dlasitap and the sun still have me confused."

The faint sound of water persisted. It was not unlike the

sound it usually made against the castle when the tides were rising or falling. 65G-849 walked out of the chamber to the stairway which spiraled up through the castle. He looked down, listening.

"The water we hear is inside, not outside, the castle!" came his electrifying announcement.

"The leak!" 6W-438 exclaimed. "The water pressure has reopened the breach!"

"Awaken Kamunioleten!" Professor Jameson told them as he and 6W-438 clattered down the eccentrically arranged steps of the spiral stairway.

Now the noise of bubbling, lapping water grew louder. It was caused by a formation of the ceiling on the lower floor where air first became trapped and then was forced out again under increased pressure, as more water flooded the gap.

"This is bad!" the professor foreboded. "The leak is much worse than before!"

"We must see if it can be stopped!" was 6W-438's hurried decision as he plunged into the rising water which surged up the stairway.

The threatening flood enveloped them as they continued on down the submerged stairs and into the cellar level. Darkness, as well as water, buried them in its mysterious folds, so that they had recourse to their body lights. Guided by the subdued beams through the murk of the flooding menace, they groped their way to where, not so many tides gone by, the visiting Emites had repaired the leak. What they saw put in their minds a common thought. Moreover, they recognized the futility of trying to stem the inrush of waters. It was only a question of time until the flood would prove a grave menace to Kamunioleten and his three Vosquentebs.

The two machine men made their way back to the stairway where lights other than their own waved at them. 19K-59, 5ZQ-35 and 948D-21 had come to meet them. All five machine men hurried up the stairs and out of the rising flood. Professor Jameson noticed that the water had risen alarmingly since he and 6W-438 had descended.

In the minds of both Zoromes lay a common conviction: this reoccurrence of the leak had been a set design rather than accident or carelessness of the Emites who had supposedly repaired it. The insidious influence and fear of Bemencanla was clearly revealed. This was evidently of his doing. As they rushed into the upper reaches of the castle, the professor told the startled and frightened Kamunioleten as much.

"It is a design on your life and those of your servitors, an arranged accident! The waters are rising fast to drown every breathing creature in the castle!"

"The leak has been enlarged!" cried 6W-438. "We found it packed with material which would wear away slowly through action of the water! Tonight it burst!"

The color had drained from the exile's face. The Vosquentebs, aroused and excited, piped in shrill nervousness and terror.

"I had thought myself more secure!" the Emite exclaimed. "Is there no escape?"

"We must climb to the highest position in the castle," was Professor Jameson's advice, "and hope that the flood will not reach there before the tide descends."

"We must turn off the air vents which force out old air during high tide!" cried Kamunioleten. "Then the water can only rise to a height where air pressure will be equalized with that of the water pressure!"

Immediately, one of the machine men sprang to the task.

"There will be no bad effects to your respiratory system, I hope," 6W-438 reminded the Emite.

"We can change the air when the tide descends."

Higher rose the water in the castle, compressing the air in the upper chambers, which remained unflooded. The tide reached its maximum height, leaving only the top floor of the sunken castle unflooded. From then on the water receded as the tide fell and released its tremendous pressure. The professor said nothing to Kamunioleten on the matter, but he feared what the results might entail to the Emite after being subjected to so great an air pressure. Well did he realize how bubbles might be formed in the Emite's blood from too rapid a reduction of atmospheric compression.

The tide dropped slowly, and the compression became less. Finally, the level fell below the apex of the stone structure, and the pressure rapidly reached normal once more. The water flowed out of the castle as it had flowed in, and now an ingress of purified air was allowed.

Misgivings assailed the professor as one of the Vosquentebs crumpled into a heap and rolled in agony on the floor, his limbs bent and constructed.

"He, like you and your other servitors, was released from the air compression too soon," Kamunioleten was told briefly. "You may suffer from it yet."

There seemed little under the circumstances that could be done for the Vosquenteb. They could only wait. In the meantime, Kamunioleten complained of dizziness and sharp pains in his head. He sat down and was seized with a strange, shivering spell.

"It is a common ailment which I recollect in my past life on the planet Earth as afflicting deep-sea divers who came to the surface too soon and divested themsevles of their diving apparatus," the professor related. "Kamunioleten and his servitors have nothing to fear unless their peculiarities of structure differ sufficiently from the human organism I once knew, so that their death from this source may be more easily contracted."

The Emite now complained of excruciating pains, especially in his joints. One Vosquenteb was affected badly, while the other two were afflicted to a lesser degree than their fellow, who rolled on the floor gasping at the sharp pains.

"Is—is it dangerous?" flashed Kamunioleten fearfully. "Is there a chance of death from this?"

"You must leave the castle before the next high tide," the professor told him. "It is probable that you will emerge from this little the worse for wear other than a temporary weakness, but too many repetitions will prove fatal."

"Leave the castle!" the Emite cried in bewilderment. "Where? Your spaceship is absent—and there is nothing here with which to make a raft; thank Bemencanla for that! And a raft would be scarcely seaworthy, for at highest tide the waves are generally vicious!"

"We must reach the higher end of the island," 6W-438 stated.

"The tides will never let us do it," Kamunioleten replied wearily as a sudden wave of sharp pain racked his body and passed. "The distance is too far to be made between ebb and flow."

"It is your only chance if you would live," said the professor. "I can truthfully tell you that a few more such experiences as this one will be the death of you."

"I can truly believe it!" the Emite exclaimed as he gripped his body at another spasm. "But I can never make it to the other end of the island, even were I feeling in the best of shape, which I am not."

The sorely afflicted Vosquenteb was still lying on the floor but was now more quiet. He groaned occasionally, but it was evident that the more evil effects of the too rapid decompression were wearing off. His companions, too, were a sickly pair, but not as bad as he, for they had not labored during the compression so intensively.

"The time to act is soon," the professor warned the Emite. "The waters are lowering."

"Soon the ground will be dry," 5ZQ-35 added.

"The next tide will soon return, too," Kamunioleten countered gloomily. "Death either way, stay or go, but I would rather die drowning than stay here for another period, or several more periods, of compression and expire in such agony as this."

"The spaceship may return soon," said 19K-59, "yet it seems a poor chance upon which to gamble."

"We shall carry you at our swiftest pace," the professor assured the Emite and his three companions.

Kamunioleten considered this hopefullly, while his three satellites did not think much on the matter at all, but more on their present discomfort and woe, ready to do almost anything that Kamunioleten bade them, especially if it were to escape the horrors occasioned by the leak in the castle.

Once more the machine men plunged into the watery depths under the castle to ascertain for a certainty that there was no possibility of repairing the leak. Such a course appeared useless. As the water flowed away from the base of the castle, the professor rapidly made his plans. Of the eight machine men, three were to remain at the castle until the spaceship returned or until the professor and his four companions returned from the upper end of the island; 948D-21, 65G-849 and 777Y-46 were detailed to remain at the castle.

Immediately, knowing that time and speed were precious, the professor and his four machine men set out for the higher end of the island at a rapid pace, carrying the three Vosquentebs and Kamunioleten. One of the Vosquentebs claimed that he could run as fast as the machine men carrying his companions, but with foresight the professor wisely bade him conserve his energies.

Over the island's perceptibly sloping surface, the machine men carried the four creatures of the twin worlds. They knew no exhaustion—only a ceaseless, mechanical toil of metal parts under the direction of an organic brain, a brain whose every need was supplied by synthetic application of material housed in the cone-shaped heads.

They were glad to find an even and unobstructed terrain, being able to thank the leveling effects of the perennial tides for this. Farther away from the vicinity of the castle, after they had traveled what Kamunioleten told them was nearly half the distance to the high tide mark, they commenced to notice small vegetable growths and a strange kind of moss growing, luxuriant and plentiful.

On they went, finding the footing in certain spots none too certain, for at this level queer little animals lived an amphibious life in the succession of ebb and flow tides, digging burrows in the ground, many of these holes being partly concealed by moss and other vegetable growths. Several times the hurrying machine men stepped in these and occasioned rough falls for their organic riders. Kamunioleten stated, however, that this uncertain progress would extend for little more than a borg, for the little water animals lived at only a certain depths of attained pressure. It seemed that their burrows remained partly filled with water at low tide, and several of the amphibians scurried out of sight from the rapid advance of the machine men and their riders, diving into their burrows from which a splash of water geysered as they disappeared from sight.

The five machine men had passed this region of the treacherous burrows when Kamunioleten gave a startled exclamation and pointed off into the distance ahead of them and to their right. A round, curved slice of pale brilliance lay upon the horizon and was slowly gaining volume.

"Dlasitap!"

The discovery caused the machine men to redouble their efforts, for they had no longer the fear of stepping into the numerous holes of the amphibians. Always, one of them remained unburdened to proceed some distance ahead and pick out the best course in the general direction of the highlands. Dlasitap was commencing to rise, and machine men, Emite and Vosquentebs all realized what this meant. There is no large loss without some small gain, and Professor Jameson became well aware of this proverbial truth as he realized that a much straighter course might now be adhered to in their race against time and tide, for the sun was nearly overhead by now and of less use in the matter of calculated direction.

Kamunioleten bewailed the fact that there was still a long distance to be covered. Far behind them they knew that the ocean level was commencing ro rise, that it would not be long before smooth, racing rollers skimmed along beneath their hurrying metal feet. The skyline now cut Dlasitap through the center, and the planet rose higher until it hung like a gigantic crescent over the thin-hazed highlands in the distance, its proportions conjuringly enhanced by the magical perspective of far-away hills. Pale and inconspicuous against the sky, other than to the anxious fugitives who fled against its ominous ascension, Dlasitap rose steadily higher like the point of an otherwise invisible minute hand of a clock, rising to a zenith of doom.

So it appeared to the Emite and the Vosquentebs. There existed no personal danger to the nigh invincible machine men, yet it sore beset them to lose their four charges on a matter of two points: a growing comradeship was primarily involved; and the machine men abhorred the prospects of failure, especially in so vital an issue as one of life and death.

V

IT WAS ONE OF THE Vosquentebs who first gave rise to a shrill cry of alarm. Looking backward, the creature raised a limb and pointed to the rear. Far behind, a barely perceptible line of varying color grew denser and more distinguishable, as all three of the Vosquentebs echoed the first alarm, setting up a weird din of cacophonic woe.

"The tide is overtaking us!" was Kamunioleten's nervous information.

From his position where he clung tightly to the cone-shaped head of 5ZQ-35, the Emite gazed at the rapidly approaching waters and then at the rising hills, within sight yet still dangerously distant.

The professor now found the terrain rougher, here and there rock formations commencing to crop out of the ground. The first roll of waters broke against the machine men's metal bodies in a much higher wave than they had expected. The professor changed their course slightly to one side and headed for a sloping ridge of rock.

"It will not be high enough," Kamunioleten warned. "There is no high water mark upon it."

"That is so," the professor agreed, "but it is sufficiently long so that if we get it behind us, the force of the rollers will be broken and progress made easier."

This the machine men found to be true, yet the professor pondered over the wisdom of it after all, for in so doing they had lost a bit of precious distance, and an elongated depression lay for a considerable distance beyond the ridge, so that the machine men wallowed and splashed in deeper water than would have been the case had they held adamantly to their original course. But they soon splashed their way out of the hollow, yet to no degree did they find themselves once more in shallow water. The tide was rising much too swiftly, and Dlasitap lay far above the horizon. It behoved the machine men to know that although the castle they had left was many miles behind, and now beneath the horizon, the main rises in altitude lay within the last few borgs they were traveling. Only lately had the upward slope become distinctly noticeable.

Progress became more difficult as progress always is through a denser medium such as water. The machine men had known only too well that this would be so.

The rising tide swept over their metal heads and about the middles of Kamunioleten and the Vosquentebs.

"We'll never make it!" cried the Emite who, now that the machine men were unable to perceive their destination, guided them mentally. "We must swim for it, and I am a poor swimmer!"

Kamunioleten might better have said that he felt in poor condition for such an arduous task. 5ZQ-35 felt the Emite rise to his full height above him as he strove to keep his head above the water. Dlasitap had not yet reached its zenith, and the waters were still rising, but now more languidly. Soon, Kamunioleten reported that he must let go and swim or else be drowned. He had risen to where he stood on the four square corners of the machine man's metal body, 5ZQ-35 curling his tentacles about the Emite's legs.

The three Vosquentebs had already abandoned their submerged retainers and were being followed by the three machine men who looked upward through the mechanical eye in the apex of their metal heads at the swirling, thrashing limbs of the creatures. Kamunioleten reported that the high tide mark now lay less than half a borg away. In his mind, the Zoromes detected a note of helpless desperation. He was not doing as well as the Vosquentebs who were, from hereditary environment, more accustomed to the art and peculiar stamina required for swimming.

Without a warning, the Emite gave a sudden, convulsive struggle and sank into the water among the machine men, a trail of bubbles marking his short descent from the surface. 6W-438 seized him and gave him an upward shove which bobbed him to the surface once more where he was seized upon by two of the Vosquentebs who supported him and swam in the water. Their progress became slowed and their exertions redoubled. There was nothing that the machine men could do other than hope that they made it.

That final half borg was made at a tremendous cost of effort and length of time. Worn out by the trial of air compression and jogging ride on the machine men, all four of the creatures were physically worn out. Kamunioleten was practically helpless, and although the three Vosquentebs relieved each other in supporting him in the water, they were all worn and fatigued. One of them, he who had suffered the worst from the too rapid air decompression, would likely have drowned despite anything the machine men might have done, had it not been for an opportune occurrence.

Dlasitap had reached its zenith and was falling toward the horizon opposite to the one from which it had risen, and the high tide had commenced to ebb. The sun, too, was lower, and this aided the recession of the water. The weary Vosquenteb finally gave out and sank helplessly into the light green depths. The professor seized him and pushed him back up again, finding that by holding the Vosquenteb's feet over his metal head he could keep the other's head above water. The machine men now held all three of the Vosquentebs once more. Kamunioleten, having lost consciousness, was upheld and kept up by the machine men. It was decided that no more progress would be made, and here they waited for the ebbing of the tide.

The recession of the waters was surprisingly rapid as both Dlasitap and the sun simultaneously eased their attraction. When the machine men's heads broke the surface of the water, they were surprised to find themselves less than two hundred yards from the high water mark which stood out damp and clear against a rising hill in the foreground. It was nearing sunset as they climbed the hill where it was decided that they rest until morning came. Rest was a superfluous requisite to the machine men, yet they were well aware that their organic allies would require recuperation.

Against the subdued brilliance of sunset's glow they saw from their low eminence a gigantic wheel upraised above the ground, dwarfed in perspective of several borgs' distance. Kamunioleten, who had just revived from the second and most alarming of his recent ordeals, told them that it was one of the great wheels used to hurl the passenger projectiles off into space toward Dlasitap.

All that night, the machine men waited beside their four

organic friends who rested upon the hill overlooking the high tide mark. The sun gone, Dlasitap shone brightly for only a short part of the earlier evening, a hanging crescent surrounded by the glittering stars, a few of which shone dimly through the twin world's atmospheric halo. Dlasitap disappeared, leaving in its place more stars which shone the brighter because of its absence.

Looking up into the night at the far-off stars, the machine men could only wonder where the spaceship was with their metal companions. Were they at that moment returning across space, or was something detaining them?

A suggestive lessening of darkness, followed by a weak flash of light, announced the coming dawn. Knowing that Kamunioleten and his three servitors could well do with all the rest they might obtain, the machine men let them slumber on undisturbed until after the sun was well into the sky. It was then that one of the Vosquentebs awoke, and, shortly after, Kamunioleten opened his eyes. The two sleeping Vosquentebs were aroused, and the nine fugitives from the fearsome tide started for the village where the wheel held towering dominance above the rows of houses around its base. As the machine men came nearer, they saw that these houses were built mostly of stone, a few of the poorer ones made of an adobe mixture which they learned was obtained from a peculiar section of the seashore at low tide.

Several Vosquentebs first discovered the party and fled in alarm at the strange apparitions of the Zoromes in company with three of their kind and the Emite. Straight into the village walked the nine from the flooded castle. Now several Emites came to meet them, a bit falteringly, summoned by the excited Vosquentebs. They recognized Kamunioleten and their apprehensions regarding the metal monsters beside him were partly vanished.

"What do you do here, Kamunioleten?" he was asked. "And what are those machine things with you?"

"I am come from the castle," replied Kamunioleten, evasive of the query concerning his metal alies.

"You have no right up at this island's end. Where did you get a boat?"

Again the exile answered only the leading question.

"The castle has sprung a leak and is flooded at high tide."

The crowd of Vosquentebs and Emites increased until nearly the entire village was assembled. There were no more than forty Emites to the Vosquenteb population of two hundred, yet it was apparent that the Emites were the accepted masters. The five machine men were regarded with suspicion, even after Kamunioleten had explained that they were creatures from another world and would harm no one who did not attempt to harm them. It was apparent to the minds of the machine men that these Emites disliked the exile and bore him ill favor. What they might have done with Kamunioleten, had the machine men not been with him, remained largely problematical, yet it would be supposed that they would have imprisoned him until word was transmitted to Bemencanla, as these Emites were his minions.

The machine men of Zor put such plans beyond their temptation by casual feats of strength, stamina and invincibility which cultivated a passive respect and fear in the days that followed, though underneath lurked currents of hate, fear and suspicion, all too plainly visible to the machine men and faintly perceived by the less receptive faculties of Kamunioleten. Here, on the upper end of the island, the machine men took up quarters and once more waited for the return of the spaceship, knowing well that as soon as it landed by the castle the three Zoromes left behind would inform 744U-21 of their whereabouts.

During the interim, the machine men examined the catapult wheel with avid interest. It was nothing more than a gigantic flywheel, geared up and fitted with a drive shaft and run by steam power. An enormous firepit yawned like a cavern underneath the huge, metal boiler whose square walls were of surprising thickness, Kamunioleten explained, to stand the terrific strain.

"We fear the bursting of the steam chamber more than we fear the breaking up of the wheel from being whirled too rapidly. The wheel is of very light metal in order to lessen the strain of centrifugal force and avoid the accidents of earlier experiments with heavier metals."

Professor Jameson found the diameter of this particular wheel to be slightly less than two hundred and ten feet. To gain the necessary speed of considerably more than two thousand miles per hour, this would call for more than five revolutions a second before the affixed projectile might be released.

The wheel was made of several large sections running diametrically, strengthened here and there quite cleverly. The latter ability the Emites had learned through bitter experience rather than by genius, for actual experience had made a mock of many of their painstaking figures. The huge sections of the wheel, the machine men learned, were made upon a distant island of Selimemigre where the best metals were found to form the strong alloy. The massive, though surprisingly light, sections were towed to their destinations on huge floats fastened behind ships.

The wheel on this island was rarely used, as was evidenced by the condition of the firepit beneath the boiler, which was cleaned and oiled to prevent deterioration. The professor suggested to Kamunioleten that their alloy be made rustproof, to which he replied that many of the wheels were coated with a rustproof preparation of metal which was applied in the molten state. He professed to know little concerning this phase of the construction other than to assert that a rustproof alloy had been made once, but was found on practical experiment to be too weak.

"Still in a rather crude state," 6W-438 said, referring to the wheel, "yet give them time."

The machine men hungered for a demonstration of the wheel, yet their curiosity remained unappeased, for there arose no occasion for its use. As they had discovered, this wheel was rarely used for its purpose of hurling miniature spacecraft between the twin worlds.

More time passed. Still the spaceship did not arrive from Dlasitap. The machine men were growing restless in the absence of their companions, especially in the face of the ever present uncertainty. Finally, Professor Jameson made an electrifying statement, a statement fraught with stirring possibilities.

"We are going to Dlasitap."

"The wheel?" cried 6W-438, rapidly divining his thoughts.

"The wheel," the professor replied.

The professor made known to Kamunioleten his intentions, and the latter not only expressed surprise, but fear and anxiety as well, anxiety for the machine men as well as for himself.

"I would not trust these fellows of mine if I were you," he warned the Zoromes. "They may send your projectile on a fatal course even as was the common fate of my Administrators."

"You will be here to superintend," the professor added, "and besides, two more of the machine men will be left here on the island with you, for not only must the wheel be well attended on our parting, but you could well fear for yourself if left alone here with the hirelings of Bemencanla."

Professor Jameson assigned 5ZQ-35 and 8L-404 to stay

with Kamunioleten and help in the operation of the wheel. The Emite knew something of the wheel's operation, especially the estimation which must necessarily be accurate to insure a safe arrival on Dlasitap. This estimation called for a choice of certain portions of Dlasitap to face Selimemigre at the time the projectile was released from the wheel. Also, the gross weight of the projectile and its occupants must be considered in connection with the speed of the revolving wheel, for the projectile might fare disastrously should it reach the other world ahead of or behind its planned schedule. A return trip did not offer so many dangers, for Selimemigre offered several more times the area of water for allowance of mistakes than did Dlasitap.

None of this would Kamunioleten and his five metal allies dare to leave to the trust, even jointly, of the Emites on the island, so Professor Jameson sent back to the castle for two of the machine men who, after the projectile had left for Dlasitap, might return to their solitary companion awaiting them at the lower end of the island.

In this manner, the three machine men who were preparing for the novel crossing of space to Dlasitap in search of the spaceship's whereabouts, now had Kamunioleten, four of their metal brethren and the three Vosquentebs to aid them in their takeoff.

Professor Jameson, 6W-438 and 19K-59 closely examined the four metal projectiles grouped in one of the smaller buildings about the base of the great wheel. With interest, they tested them, and with the Emite's suggestions made their selection. Rapidly, they learned the few requirements necessary for what little operation the projectile would need as they fell upon Dlasitap.

The fanwise atmosphere brakes were found to be in excellent working order, ready to be unfolded from the miniature spaceship at the proper moment, while the light metal parachute was also found to be in easy working order. A test was given the heating system of the projectile, and as a preliminary to starting, the projectile was well fueled, this latter requisite also being essential to the steamdriving power, readily attached when the projectile bobbed to the surface of one of Dlasitap's larger bodies of water.

Timid and distrustful of this pioneering, crude travel of the Emites, Kamunioleten expressed his fears at the same time he was wishing the three Zoromes a successful trip.

"You made the trip once without mishap," the professor reminded him.

Kamunioleten's pessimism remained undaunted.

"But I was making the trip the safer way—to Selimemigre, not to Dlasitap. If I recollect right, the actual destination of our projectile failed by some seventy borgs or more the position our senders had selected for us to come down, but the nearest land lay a good hundred and ninety borgs away—one of the larger islands—and so the mistake amounted to naught." And here the Emite added a bit of possible cheer to what was otherwise a revelation of dismal possibilities. "It may be that our senders estimated roughly and without due care because they knew of our comparative safety in the vast expanse of water for which we were headed."

VI

THE TRIP MECHANISM for releasing the projectile from its straining hold on the rim of the giant wheel was located at the outer end of a long arm extending from the gearhousing of the massive axle. From below, a towering drive shaft loomed gigantically out of the lesser compartments attached to the squat steam compressor. Like the light yet amazingly strong alloy comprising the wheel itself, this drive shaft's composition was constituted similarly, though with a varying regard for friction in parts where friction ensued, despite lubrication.

The Emite and the machine men carefully made their calculations; then they waited for the day to come when the position and surface of Dlasitap would be most opportunely situated. They had but little more than two days to wait, when at high tide the time for the crossing was at hand. Kamunioleten, wishing the three metal adventurers well, expressed his relief that he was not going with them, in spite of his strong desire to return again to the home from which he had been exiled.

With something akin to excitement, Professor Jameson, 6W-438 and 19K-59 watched the three Vosquentebs fueling the fire pit beneath the steam compressor, which held just the right amount of water. The Emite, giving them his final farewell and best wishes, bade them enter the projectile and screw down the hatch. From several transparent facings, the three Zoromes looked out upon the further proceedings, or what could be seen of them through the blurred window composition, its defective condition caused by inner and outer hulls of the projectile to retain the heat of the craft and restrict the effects of unveiled sunlight. These transparent facings could be covered from within at will.

Smoke arose from the firepit, around which the Vosquentebs scampered excitedly in the gathering glow like rejoicing imps before an inferno. Kamunioleten with two of the machine men were out of sight in the nearby building where steam pressure was regulated. There was an interval of waiting.

A cloud of steam burst suddenly from around the base of the towering drive shaft, its loud hiss unheard by the three machine men inside the projectile at the bottom of the motionless wheel. High above, on the roof of the gear-housing, stood 8L-404, his tentacles ready at the trip, prepared to release the whirling projectile at the precise moment when he was signaled from below. All about the wheel, standing at a respectful distance, stood the inhabitants of the island, Emites and Vosquentebs.

"Soon, the wheel will start turning." 777Y-46's mental note penetrated the metal projectile. "Be sure you have the straps secure about yourselves."

The three Zoromes glanced quickly at each other across the narrow confines of the projectile. It was shaped like a short hallway of their own space ship. A tiny compartment operating the mechanism lay in the rear, while up in the prow was stored fuel and supplies, including the navigation facilities for making the projectile into a steam-driven boat when they reached Dlasitap. They had no use for the air rejuvenator, and they would have had no need for the heating equipment if they had possessed their headgear for temperature equalizing, but, as it was, this latter equipment lay aboard the missing spaceship, and so a small amount of heat would be necessary later on when their present supply of natural heat waned.

As they had calculated, Dlasitap would rotate completely some three times or more before they crossed the hundred thousand miles of space separating the twin worlds. They would leave for Dlasitap traveling close to twenty-five hundred miles per hour, according to the professor's condensation of Kamunioleten's borgs and whegs. They would slow to nearly zero halfway to Dlasitap; then the speed would once more accelerate as they dropped toward it, giving them somewhat of a two thousand mile per hour average for the entire trip.

There came a perceptible motion, and the scenery moved

slowly, distortingly, through the crude transparency. It was like the initial rise in a ferris wheel at a county fair. This similarity struck the professor across the scarcely conceivable abyss of forty million years. He noticed a gradual change of gravity, for, unlike the recollected ferris wheel, the projectile remained immovable on the immense rim. Scenery flew by faster until it became no longer distinguishable, the accelerating revolutions resolving into a blinking alternation of bright sky and grayish, purple land and foliage, the lesser green spots merged into obscurity.

Then the professor noted further that there was no longer a change in gravity: there was but one gravity, and in but one direction, and that was outward, the synthetic gravity induced by centrifugal force.

Faster and faster the wheel flew. Soon, they would be making about five revolutions per second, providing the necessary component to send them flying out of Selimemigre's gravitational attraction at a speed greater than that with which they would proceed toward Dlasitap, slowly losing momentum until they passed through neutral territory.

Suddenly upon their senses there burst the telepathic cry of 8L-404.

"Now—be ready! You leave for Dlasitap!"

Gravity quickly altered its position. From one side of the projectile it shifted to the base. Only in this manner did these three machine men realize that they had been released from the giant flywheel. Yet the professor also noticed that the flickering changes of light and shadow previously seen through the ports now yielded to a steady filter of soft light, and this, while he was considering it, dulled into darkness as the projectile rushed rapidly out of the atmosphere, guided unerringly by stabilizer fins.

They were in space, launched on their hundred thousand mile journey at an initial momentum close to twenty-five hundred miles per hour.

Peering out of one of the windows, the professor bent forward from his straps to note the position of Dlasitap. Relief smote him, for one of their chief worries was removed. The projectile was headed in the right direction, though not directly for the great globe, being aimed ahead of its course so that the focal point of attraction beyond the field of neutral gravity would coincide with Dlasitap's current position at that fateful moment.

"We can remove our straps now," said 6W-438. "Let us take a look around."

It was scarcely an unfamiliar panorama which lay about them; it was rather a warped vision, however, due to the crude qualities of the observation facings. Selimemigre, what little could be seen of it from ports designed almost exclusively for side and forward observation, loomed huge in their rear. On all sides and ahead lay the fiery firmament with Dlasitap growing slowly gibbous ahead and slightly to one side of their course.

The machine men now commenced a patient wait, not without anxiety, for their projectile to come in close to Dlasitap. The better than twenty-five hundred mile rate, which was already beginning to slow up from the tremendous pulling bulk of Selimemigre behind, seemed agonizingly slow to the three Zoromes who were familiar with cosmic speeds many times faster. To record the passing of time, they took occasional glimpses of Dlasitap's topography, the slowly moving continental masses serving as the figures of their celestial clock.

Patience was an accomplishment among the metal Zoromes, yet in this insecure and helpless position they remained a bit on edge. What if the projectile were not aimed at the right spot ahead of Dlasitap's present position? Worse, and more probable than missing the twin world entirely, was the likely hazard of hitting solid land instead of the ocean depths which they had been carefully timed to hit. The professor could not help but dwell on this discomforting thought, roundly denouncing his impatience at the delayed return of the spaceship. Here he had placed himself and his two metal companions in what might well prove to be an uncompromising alliance with death. Here was scarcely wisdom but another impulsive and adventurous gesture such as his entrance into the transition cube of the Tripeds. Yet he argued with himself that the circumstances surrounding the failure of that spaceship to return were reason enough for his choice of courses. He recollected well his timely arrival on the island of light at the center of the hydrosphere's hollowed core, discovering 744U-21 and several more metal companions in dire straits. The possibilities in this situation promised to be much the same.

The professor's conscience, however, remained unsatisfied despite the obvious and seemingly incontrovertible logic which he had offered himself so convincingly. Behind this logic there lurked the unquenchable spirit of adventure ever ready to force him and his companions into any novel experience, represented in this instance by the giant flywheel and its unguided missile now hurtling through space toward Dlasitap. In the background of this colorful venture lurked the storm of tragedy waiting to loose its thunder of destruction and lightning of death. Kamunioleten's tragic philosophy had not been one to fill them with the sense of security and fatalism they generally employed.

With agonizing slowness, Dlasitap made a complete rotation. By this time the three Zoromes found it necessary to commence operation of the heating system; the temperature would have already frozen either the Emites or Vosquentebs. 19K-58 remarked upon the lessening of gravity in their rear, and soon the machine men were able to float about their limited confines like windblown feathers in a dense atmosphere. This, as Dlasitap slowly loomed larger, resolved itself into a slight gravitational attraction at their prow. Meanwhile, Dlasitap had made its second complete rotation since they had left Selimemigre. Whatever fears they might have entertained regarding the possibilities of falling back upon Selimemigre due to the lack of a sufficiently strong push had now vanished.

This latter fear was now replaced by the apprehension that their initial push might have been too great. This exigency involved the likelihood of missing the spot on Dlasitap at which they had been aimed, or else the risk of super-momentum, in which case their brakes and parachute attachment stood in danger of being wrenched free of the tiny craft. Both could easily happen, and the professor found dissatisfaction with present interplanetary travel of the Emites. What they needed most was maneuverability in space.

"We have not long to wait," the professor observed, reflecting a bit of the nervous waiting shared by his companions.

It was this waiting, the slow rate of interplanetary speed, an average of merely two thousand miles per hour which irked them. They had all faced more desperate circumstances in the late space war with the Mumes, with less regard for their futures than now. But those encounters had been swift and decisive. There had been little waiting. Coupled with the delay of landing on Dlasitap, they were faced with the knowledge that what little control they possessed over the projectile must be held suppressed until almost the final moment.

They were picking up speed once more, regardless of the fact that the increase went unnoticed. Yet they knew it to be so, and Dlasitap grew large before them. The profes-

49

sor was glad that the projectile had not turned about during the time they had left the atmosphere of Selimemigre, although the stabilizer fins would have righted this on their entrance into the air envelope of Dlaritap. The prow pointed directly at the center of Dlasitap, and there would be no delay in the use of an air brake preceding the parachute's release.

At the controls in the small rear compartment 6W-438 strapped himself securely against the forward pull of Dlasitap's attraction. 19K-59 and the professor strapped themselves in the middle of the slim cylinder, where contact with the walls might be avoided on their landing, yet where they might see what lay ahead. They had not long to wait.

Down they hurtled toward Dlasitap. A faint haze replaced the jet blackness of space with its twinkling stars. Kamunioleten had told them that their first encounter with the atmosphere of Dlasitap would find them over a hundred miles high. The professor had figured beforehand that, at their rate of speed, a rough two and a half minutes would elapse before they reached the world's surface. This time must be lengthened considerably, if they were to effect a safe landing, by use of the air brake and metal parachute.

"The air brake!" the professor cried, peering down at the bulging surface of Dlasitap whose curvature merged more and more into the horizon as the projectile screamed and wailed through the atmosphere in its furious descent.

The machine men felt themselves jerked so hard that they pondered momentarily how organic creatures like the Emites could ever live through such an ordeal. 6W-438's release of the air brake had been consummated much too swiftly, however, so much too swiftly that for a moment he was left dazed from a smash of his metal head against the partition behind him, a blow sufficient to have broken any skull comprised of bone.

Transecting the rear of the projectile, a broad, flat disk constructed of segmented, interlocking metal staves, hastily released, braked their rapid speed through the increasing density of air. Professor Jameson looked anxiously downward for the ocean. It seemed as if they must strike, for the headland lay directly below.

"The metal parachute! Release it!"

6W-438 did not hear the order. He had not yet fully emerged from his shock of contact with the partition. Dangling loosely in their straps, several of which had been snapped at the sudden yank of the air brake, the professor and 19K-59 desperately regarded their swiftly impending fate.

"The parachute!" Professor James echoed. "Quick!"

It was into the mind of 6W-438 that these anxious thoughts gradually crept, clearing his torpid senses and sending a tentacle flashing to a pair of long handles which he turned rapidly. Behind the slim, metal bullet, a pleated column of thin metal unhinged itself and, caught by the wailing winds, quickly grew cone-shaped like the head of the machine men themselves. Once more the three Zoromes surged forward in their straps, a hurried glimpse of the professor's confirming his worst fears. They were rushing down upon the edge of the rocky headland where water and beach merged into foam.

"We shall crash!" was 19K-59's terrifying emanation.

Less than five miles lay between them and death, and this respite was being rapidly eaten by the rushing projectile as it tore madly through the air. Another quick observation gave him a sudden spark of hope.

"We have sideswiped!" he told his metal companions. "The parachute's imperfections are throwing us a bit to one side of a vertical fall!"

"Not in time!" was 19K-59's foreboding. "The water, even if we do strike it, will be too shallow!"

6W-438, in the partitioned rear, could not see forward and said nothing, attending the scanty controls according to the observations of his companions.

Land rushed upward, land and water. Now they were so close that even 6W-438 could distinguish their proximity.

"Shall I let go the parachute?" he exclaimed, remembering Kamunioleten's final instructions

To retain the parachute as they struck meant a rupture of the projectile even if they hit water. But Professor Jameson had already made his gamble with fate.

"No! Keep it!"

VII

WITH A TERRIFIC IMPACT, they struck. The remaining straps were broken from the professor and 19K-59, hurling them into a tangled heap among the fuel supplies of the forward compartment. Almost simultaneously there came another terrific shock, and as the professor's senses left him in a bright flash of light, the interrupted thought smote his mind that they had struck in shallow water.

The truth of the matter was too swiftly consummated for the brief consciousness of Professor Jameson to fully apprehend. They had indeed struck shallow water, but not as shallow as his ebbing thoughts had conceived. The second impact was no less than the trailing parachute jerking their dive to a less hazardous speed as it caught the water.

6W-438 came to his senses and looked about him. His first conception was the vague sensation that he was lying in water. Zoromes possessing scarcely any sense of touch beyond tangible contact, or a change in solids, this divination was truly remarkable. He affirmed this supposition as consciousness gave his brain access to mechanical eyesight. Something weighed him down, and from off him he shoved some of the wreckage of the metal parachute.

He rose to his feet and found himself mechanically uninjured. In the clear water all about him, and far out of sight over his head, swam fishes of various sorts, a few darting curiously in and about the wreckage of the projectile. He looked about him for 21MM392 and 19K-59. Not until he had peered beneath broken sections from the projectile did he realize that not only were his metal companions gone but also the entire forward section of the interplanetary projectile. He now fully understood that it had broken apart when the parachute had struck the water.

His companions and the rest of the wreckage were somewhere else. He turned slowly and looked in every direction. Finally, several hundred feet off, he saw what was left of the forward section. It lay crumpled, the metal legs and lower half of a metal cube extending from under it. 6W-438 slowly approached, and as he did so he saw the other machine man lying half buried in the mud a few yards from the wreckage. It was 19K-59, while under the semi-remains of the projectile lay 21MM392.

19K-59 stirred himself and arose amid a cloud of muddy water. Together, he and 6W-438 dragged the professor out from under the wreckage.

"Is he dead?" queried 19K-59, his brain still muddled from the swift succession of events and the subsequent crash.

"I do not know," 6W-438 replied fearfully. "His head seems undamaged, yet—"

They examined the professor. His body had lost a tentacle, and one leg was slightly bent yet still usable. 19K-59, it seemed had been thrown clear. Both Zoromes carefully probed the professor's brain with their own thoughts. His own brain structure, unless left open for reception, had always been a difficult one for the Zoromes to penetrate, but if any of them had learned this art to particular advantage over their fellows it was 6W-438. A glad exclamation escaped his mind as he felt signs of life in the professor's mind.

Patiently, he and 19K-59 waited, and sure enough, after a lengthy interval 21MM392 came to his senses and slowly got to his feet. For a moment he recollected nothing, and then memory returned.

"What happened?" he asked.

"The projectile broke into two parts when the parachute caught hold of the water," 6W-438 told him. "I sank with the back compartment, 19K-59 was thrown clear, while you fell with the front section."

"We must get to dry land," the professor stated as he gathered his faculties once more.

"How deep do you suppose this water is?" 19K-59 ventured.

"It is difficult to tell," 6W-438 replied, looking upward through the eye in the apex of his conical head. "Due to the unusual brightness, it would not seem to be very deep, but the water is quite clear, and we may be in very deep water."

"Look for the incline toward land," the professor instructed. "I wonder how far away, and in what direction, that headland rises out of the water."

"It cannot be far," 6W-438 stated, "if what I remember from my final observation is correct."

As the machine men walked, the water grew darker, and they knew that daylight was slowly ebbing in this hemisphere. After dark, they still continued aimlessly until they realized futility.

"We could wander erratically for a long time over the ocean bed and never get anywhere," the professor remarked. "There are no landmarks or celestial objects by which to set a course."

So they waited for daylight which was later in coming here in the watery depth. They were only roughly aware of how much water lay above their heads, the professor computing it to be less than a hundred feet, though he was not certain of this. There was one encouragement: the pressure of the water grew lighter, and they knew that they were approaching shallower depths.

Another night came and passed. They did no walking

53

during the night; then resumed their search for the shore with morning. Often they climbed what appeared to be knolls on the sea bottom. They came across all sorts of marine life, sea life in strange, fantastic forms. On one of these knolls, they were near enough to discern the surface above them. As an experiment, they climbed each upon the other, yet the surface lay out of their reach, and no observations could be taken.

They discussed the direction they would take. Already, they had done much fruitless wandering. While they pondered the possibilities, the water grew darker. It seemed too soon for late afternoon twilight, and the three Zoromes looked up to see a dark object hovering above them. Into the mind of Professor Jameson flashed a memory of the huge fish which had swallowed 88ZQ4 and himself when they had sunk into the depths of the hydrosphere, yet this shadowy object above them moved too mechanically and majestically to be a fish. Moreover, its movement was too sluggish for association with the marine denizens.

"A boat!" flashed 6W-438.

"Quick—climb up on me and seize hold of the bottom!" the professor decided rapidly as the keel swept low over their heads, just out of reach.

6W-438 was the first to mount and curl his tentacles about a contrivance serving as a rudder. It could be better termed a steering arrangement, for it in no way resembled a rudder such as Professor Jameson had known on Earth. 19K-59 was next to be assisted by the professor from below and by 6W-438 from above. Last, the professor leaped upward and seized the helping tentacles of his metal companions to be hauled to a position where he, too, could command a secure hold.

"This is our best chance of making dry land," he told them. "Sooner or later, this ship of theirs will put into a harbor."

"It may be a long trip."

"But we are sure of a destination."

Resolutely, the three Zoromes clung. They could climb no higher, or they would have boarded the boat. It was deemed the better part of discretion not to make their presence known unless they were able to board, for they had no knowledge of what measures those on the boat might take. They strained their intellects for information from the minds of those above. This they finally learned: they were

54

on a commercial boat bound for Onolekag, and the boat was rapidly nearing its destination.

"It is a seaport city," the professor remarked, remembering what Kamunioleten had told him, "a seaport on the ocean for which we were aimed, if my geography of Dlasitap serves me right."

From above the machine men, the dull, throbbing sound of mechanism reached them, yet on either side of the boat they saw the water disturbed by long sweeps which propelled the vessel forward, the latter suggestive of organic labor.

The light waned, and darkness came early in the watery depths. All afternoon, they had seen the bottom of the sea sliding past beneath them, their only gauge of progress. Strange to say, the water had not grown shallower, though according to the thought transmissions received from the deck they were rapidly making port. It was evident on second consideration that the vessel was keeping to the deeper lanes of travel near the seacoast, and that their previous passage through the shallower waters had either been unavoidable or else was a mistake on the part of the pilot.

Night fell, and when dawn followed, the waters commencing to grow murky with light, the three submerged stowaways found the sweeps at rest and the vessel slowly drifting. The mechanism still labored above but with a subdued note to its voice. For some time during the darkness, the machine men had been aware of an abatement in speed.

While they considered the situation and sought to probe the minds of those above them, something shot overboard, ploughing the depths and followed by a streamer of tiny bubbles which fought their way back to the surface. In the growing light, they saw a great weight settle on the bottom, a weight to which was attached a long line.

"We must be in the harbor of Onolekag," said the professor, peering down at the smooth bottom below them. "We shall investigate. Stay here. 19K-59, while 6W-438 and I look for shore. If we become lost from the boat and do not find shore, guide us back. If we find shore, we shall call to you."

This precaution, though wise, was found to be scarcely necessary, for the two machine men wandered into shallower water along rough, rocky columns supporting the docks of Onolekag. They announced their discovery to 19K-59, who soon joined them. The three Zoromes quickly found their way out from under the dock and emerged from the water on a stony beach. From this place they had their first view of Dlasitap, of the surface of that world.

In the early morning sunlight, they looked out upon the harbor of Onolekag where several boats lay at rest upon the water. Several Emites moved busily about the dock at this early hour, not yet having noticed the three machine men who had slipped quietly out of the water. The latter were at a loss to pick out the boat which had brought them, but the mystery of the sweeps and accompanying sound of mechanism was explained.

The long oars were operated by a steam engine. A long drive shaft between decks worked back and forth, performing the movement of a long oval, lifting the sweeps out of the water on the under path of movement and pushing them against the water on the upper travel. One of the smaller boats just setting out from the dock gave demonstration of their smooth working efficiency.

Suddenly their attention was distracted from the boats by a cry from the rear. An Emite had seen them and was calling the attention of all near and far to the strange sight the three Zoromes presented as they walked slowly to the dock. Some of the Emites ran in terror, adding to the general chattering din, while others advanced, half fearful yet curious. The machine men radiated their thoughts, attempting to placate the apprehensions of the Emites. This they did, partially, yet distrust and lingering suspicion prevailed.

"Have you never seen or heard of anything like us?" the professor asked, indirectly seeking word of the space-ship.

It was evident that sight of the machine men was something new for the Emites, nor had they ever heard of them.

"We are from another world," the professor told them.

This information was immediately seized upon by the Emites and relayed into the reference to "thinking machines" from another world of their planetary system, a world other than Selimemigre.

"Enitizes, your grand capital of Dlasitap, is not far from here—not more than seventy-five borgs, is it?" the professor asked.

The affirmation was immediately provoked in the minds of the Emites, who marveled that these mechanical thinkers

56

should be from another world and still know so much about the private affairs of Dlasitap.

"We wish to go to Enitizes," the professor asserted, avoiding information of the fact that they were come from the twin world of Selimemigre.

In this desire they were to be satisfied sooner and more elaborately than they could have expected. Out of the city a military detachment came running, surrounding them and forcing them into a boat. Word had passed into the city that enemies from another world had come to Dlasitap. Coincident with their plans to go to Enitizes, the machine men found that they were being transported there aboard ship as prisoners, for Onolekag had no place to keep them.

This had all been done so rapidly as to surprise the three Zoromes, who, as their desires were being consummated, submitted peacefully. But from their captors' minds they stole information bit by bit during the trip to Enitizes, learning that a few of the nations of Dlasitap were straining at diplomatic relations, and armed forces were ready for any hostilities which might arise. The weapons of the Emites, they discovered later, were not unlike short rifles, which, under air compression, shot forth small pellets of explosives which detonated against whatever they happened to strike. 6W-438 was hit by one when an overzealous Emite forced him back from the edge of the boat where he had been regarding the operation of the mechanical sweeps. No damage, beyond a slight blackening of a metal leg where the pellet had exploded, was suffered by him.

Shortly after sunset, they rode into the harbor of the great city of Enitizes, an international city of Dlasitap, where the world government held forth in all its pomp and power. The city was not only larger than the one they had just left, but it boasted more pretentious buildings.

Without ceremony, the three machine men were escorted to the city's museum where their metal legs were chained to the gigantic cube of rock on which they stood for the curious eyes of the Emites. Nearly the entire populace of Enitizes thronged the great hall, coming and going during the next few days in order to see the strange thinking machines from another world. The three Zoromes regarded the chains in secret amusement, especially the professor, for in his foretentacle he carried a heat ray with such intensive power that it would melt through these light metal alloy chains as if they were no more than hempen cords. For the time being, they were willing to submit to these measures, searching the minds of those who came for an inkling of the lost spaceship and its occupants.

"Where do you suppose it is?" 19K-59 opened the question uppermost in the minds of the three.

"An accident out in space, perhaps," 6W-438 suggested. "They may be somewhere out in space at this moment still making repairs."

"It is more likely that they have landed on Dlasitap in some isolated spot," siad the professor. "In a few more days, unless we find out where they are, we shall leave this place and discover what transportation facilities exist for a search on other parts of Dlasitap."

Several more days passed. The throngs of curious Emites did not diminish in numbers, for the report of the thinking machines had spread afar, and many were coming from other cities to see the strange creatures. The machine men remained aloof and uncommunicative, much to the chagrin of the various Emites who were most scientifically curious, but it was generally understood that they were from a distant world and that their spaceship had fallen into the ocean.

The machine men were interested to learn that the Administrators were soon coming in a body to view the metal curiosities that had been so easily captured. Great preparations were made ready for the honored visit, and a broad dais with luxurious seats was built directly before the three curious exhibits. The seats could scarcely be called chairs by the professor, who noted their peculiar structure adapted especially for the four-legged creatures.

On the day looked forward to, the great hall was crammed to its utmost capacity with Emites, and the seven Administrators, true to universal form, magnified their pomp and importance by a late arrival. The building echoed and re-echoed to the acclaiming din, and, also universal in custom, the occasion called for a speech. It was from no less than Bemencanla himself.

VIII

THE MACHINE MEN found that he differed little superficially from the general run of Emites, but within his mind they readily discerned the turbulent, treacherous currents of avarice, cunning and hypocrisy. Bemencanla's speech ran true to form. It was flowery, exuded patriotism and honor,

58

and cited the magnificent progress under the recent regime, utterly ignoring the strained ties which now existed among several of the nations. The Grand Administrator reached a point where, in quivering wrath, he referred to the demise of the previous regime.

"And Kamunioleten, that arch-criminal who so ingloriously brought his comrades to an untimely death, should no longer reap a profitable luxury in exile on Selmemigre! Legislation should be, and now is, in the making for his execution, a long delayed justice to the rights of our citizenry! One who would cast his fellow Administrators to meet death in space in order to achieve his own selfish ends is no longer fit to live, either on Dlasitap or Selimemigre!"

As Bemencanla paused for breath and to instill a greater significance to his words, another voice interrupted, a silent voice that gripped the minds of the assembled thousands.

"Those last are the truest words you have spoken! But in those words you have not described Kamunioleten but yourself! You, Bemencanla, were the one who planned the hideous crime you have just described, planning it so cleverly as to cover Kamunioleten with the blame!"

This message rang like a siren in the minds of the gathered Emites. In Bemencanla's words, Professor Jameson, irked by the past few days of inactivity and lack of information regarding his lost companions, recognized the opportune moment. He paused in the midst of the gasp which went up from the stricken Emites, as they realized that from this walking mechanism had issued a vibrant denunciation of Bemencanla. The Grand Administrator's face blanched, while the mouth on the top of his head fell open in dumb surprise and consternation. The professor continued, citing, in clear thought pictures and mental suggestion, the entire perfidy of Bemencanla and the injustice done to Kamunioleten. It was all done so rapidly that in the hush of surprise there was little time for action. Bemencanla was the first to recover.

"A lie—a great lie!" he shrieked. "These metal things are an invention of Kamunioleten flung across space to finish the ruin he commenced! Destroy them! They must be destroyed at once!"

The spell was broken. The guards surrounding the Administrators' stand shoved their way toward the block of stone on which the machine men stood chained. From a curling tentacle of one, they saw a dazzling, blinding light throw its aura about the chains that bound it. Before

59

they realized what was happening, they saw the machine man free of the chains and at work on those which held his companions. Several chugging sounds were followed by small explosions about the body of the Zorome who worked unscathed and little perturbed by the guns of the approaching guards.

Entirely free of the chains, the three machine men waited for the guards who, with more bravery than good sense, mounted the block of stone to overwhelm them. There followed more firing of guns before they came to grips, and then the machine men picked up their recent captors and hurled them out into the excited, milling throng, whose combined voices were throwing the place into an uproar that made the building tremble.

"How are we to get out of here into the open?" 6W-438 queried.

"Follow me," was the reply.

Adjusting his heat ray to low intensity, Professor Jameson leveled it at that section of the throng opposing their passage to the nearest exit. Badly burned, the screaming Emites opened a lane by scrambling out of harm's way over the heads of their more fortunate neighbors. Out of the museum and into the city avenue ran the machine men of Zor, still undecided on a course. From near and far came running thousands of the Emites, attracted by the uproar.

"What about the dock?" 6W-438 suggested. "They can overcome us by sheer weight of numbers here. We can either steal one of their boats or else hide in the ocean."

But now the machine men were at a loss as to the direction in which the harbor lay. 19K-59 believed he knew the way, and they ran in that direction, only to meet a wall of excited Emites, aroused and brandishing various types of weapons.

"Remember the Aytans!" cried 6W-438. "We must not let them snare us!"

The machine men turned and ran down another thoroughfare. Soon they met another wave of the creatures, several hundred strong, choking the street as far as they could see. Again they made a right-hand turn into the path of least resistance. This course brought them into the vicinity of what the machine men took to be industrial buildings. Ahead of them they saw no resistance, yet behind and farther away on either side they could hear the din of the menacing mobs.

"They are herding us!" the professor warned. "This way is too easy!"

"How could they have become organized against our escape so quickly?" interjected 6W-438.

This question remained unanswered as the machine men hurried onward. With sudden despair, they saw a yelling horde break into the avenue from both sides just ahead, having emerged from the opening leading into the now solid succession of buildings. Behind them they heard and saw strange vehicles, each carrying fully a dozen of the Emites and all bearing down upon them.

"Into this building!" Professor Jameson urged his metal comrades. "We are not caught yet!"

The three Zoromes ducked quickly into a broad opening at the base of a nearby building. Inside, huge masses of mechanism testified to their recent guess that they were in an industrial center. Hasty glances showed them that the Emites were still pursuing. 6W-438 talked desperately of making a stand, realizing at the same time its futility unless they could discover a position of advantage.

Through the long dimly lighted factory, the Emites pursued the machine men. At the far end waited more of them, biding quietly. 19K-59 was first to see them in the gloom ahead, and he gave warning.

"There is no way to turn!" 6W-438 exclaimed.

"Here!" The professor suited his thought with action as he climbed rapidly up the incline of a towering piece of machinery. "Up here!"

6W-438 and 19K-59 scrambled after, as the professor paused to repel the advancing mob with his heat ray. This time the heat ray was increased to damaging intensity. One of the foremost of the Emites who clambered in pursuit fell back upon his companions semi-decapitated, a black, charred area marking the recent position of his head. The professor now swung the formidable weapon in a slow circling arc as he and his mechanical brethren climbed to a position where it was impossible to go higher.

"Are we secure here, do you think?" 19K-59 asked.

"As secure here as anywhere else until we can manage to reach the harbor and hide beneath the water," said the professor. "We can lose them easily there."

"And ourselves as well," 6W-438 added.

A barrage of gunfire broke out and a splatter of explosions all around the machine men dazzled them momentarily. With the exception of a mechanical eye destroyed

61

in the head of 19K-59, the machine men suffered no harm, clamping shut their optical shutters until the firing was over.

Professor Jameson expressed his belief: "They'll find a way to subdue us unless we can get safely to the harbor."

"Shall we make a break?"

"Nightfall will soon come. Let us defend this position until then."

During the lull in hostilities, several Emites came pushing their way through the crowd below, evidently being in some authority by the way they were given immediate passage. They came as near as they dared to the foot of the great piece of mechanism and its besieged Zoromes, stopping outside the ring of dead Emites strewn on the floor. They gave vent to unintelligible jargon directed at the machine men, the latter disregarding the sound entirely, concentrating their faculties upon the mental waves of the Emites.

"Owmitelverol has expressed his wishes that you be heard through in peace regarding the denunciations you made against Bemencanla, the Grand Administrator. No harm will come to you during the interview."

This last promise, though temporarily reassuring, was an ominous one. The professor considered, then turned to his metal companions.

"It offers a slightly better chance than this one." He gestured at their present position. "Let us see Owmitelverol and talk with him."

"We can prove nothing," cautioned 6W-438, who yet recognized in this new measure an increased opportunity for escape.

"We can only state the facts squarely, see what effect they take and then afterward act accordingly," the professor stated.

The machine men were escorted to the Grand Administration Building, where they were left under guard. Their interview with Owmitelverol was scheduled for the following morning.

During the interview, a murmur had arisen from many throats in the street below, swelling to a roar of excitement and confusion. Disturbed, Owmitelverol went to a window to ascertain the cause of the disorder, aware of the fact that all three machine men were in his presence, leaving none of them responsible for the present tumult in the streets below. Professor Jameson pressed to the window. A huge shape settled slowly into the public square.

"The spaceship!"

Leaving Owmitelverol still staring out of the window in dumb surprise, the three Zoromes clattered down the innumerable steps and out into the milling crowds of Emites surrounding the spaceship at a respectful distance. Recklessly, they pushed their way toward the ship which they were so glad to see once more, especially at such an alarming time. As they burst into the wide opening given the spaceship by the awed Emites, out of the ship came a machine man closely followed by several metal companions. It was 744U-21, and behind him came 948D-21, oneof those the professor had left at the flooded castle where Kamunioleten had spent his exile. To their surprise and the greater surprise of the already astounded Emites, Kamunioleten himself, smiling and excited, emerged from the spaceship.

But this astonishment, though the greatest one to overwhelm the staring Emites, was surpassed by the sight which now greeted the professor as five machine men followed in the wake of Kamunioleten. There should have been nothing so particularly surprising about them had it not been for the striving departure in the shape of their heads, which were not at all conical but were long and cylindrical, rounded on the top and possessing fewer mechanical eyes than the usual number encircling the coned superstructures of the machine men.

"Where have you been so long, 744U-21?" Professor Jameson queried in open amazement. "And what is the matter with their heads?"

"I conceived a better plan after the spaceship was less than halfway to Dlasitap," 744U-21 explained. "I took careful calculations as to where the lost projectile with its five Administrators would be and set out to find it. The search was more difficult than I had expected, but despite the fact that seven of Dlasitap's years had fled by since the projectile had sped off into space, we finally discovered it. The projectile was still speeding off into space at its last calculated rate of travel when astronomers here on Dlasitap eventually lost sight of it. We found it about forty-six million of your miles distant from Dlasitap, 21MM392, and still on its way toward the outer planet of this system."

"And these new machine men are the five Administrators?" the professor asked. "You brought them back to life and placed their brains in machines?"

"Yes, 21MM392, even as we did for you once," 744U-21 affirmed. "You will notice that their peculiarly shaped brains required a different cranial structure. This took a good deal of our time."

"But what of the crew of three who accompanied the Administrators?" Professor Jameson asked. "What happened to them?"

One of the new machine men answered this question himself.

"There was no crew. The crew members were in on the plan to destroy us. As soon as we found ourselves sealed alone inside the projectile and raced prematurely around the wheel we knew that all was not well. We were thrown helplessly into space with all Dlasitap believing that a crew of three accompanied us."

The ensuing excitement on Dlasitap can be well imagined. Bemencanla and several of his cohorts disappeared in some strange manner. In the meantime, a worldwide search was made for the three Emites who were to have been the crew of the fateful projectile. One of them was found, and from him was extorted the proof of Bemencanla's perfidious plot. They also learned that only a day before Bemencanla and his implicated subordinates had entered a projectile for flight to Selimemigre where Bemencanla was seeking refuge.

It was the idea of Professor Jameson to overtake them and bring them back to justice, and the suggestion was warmly acclaimed by a wrathful world. The Administrators, even ancient Owmitelverol, boarded the spaceship with the Zoromes, and off they went in search of the escaping Bemencanla. Kamunioleten showed none of his previous qualms toward interplanetary flight aboard the spaceship of Zor. As he remarked to the professor, he felt much safer where he was than where Bemencanla was.

And well might he have felt more secure, for with the directions they had been given on Dlasitap by their terrified informant, they quickly found the projectile on its way to Selimemigre.

"We can pick it up with a magnetic attracter," the professor told the Administrators, "and bring it back to Dlasitap."

"Wait!" cried one of the cylindrical-headed men, one of the Administrators who had died a slow, lingering death in the dark, lonely wastes of space. "I have a better way. Why should we not pronounce judgment against him and his conspirators right here and also execute the judgment?"

"What do you mean?" asked 744U-21, possessing only a slight inkling of the other's design.

"Let us deflect the course of the projectile so that it will be headed into the sun."

Scared faces were dimly distinguishable through the thick windows of the projectile as the space ship of Zor rode alongside and gently bumped the projectile, giving it a mighty push and multiplying its speed by a million times or better.

"What would have taken many years will now be accomplished in a matter of less than a day's time," 41C-98 observed to one of the mechanical Administrators.

Leaving the speeding projectile with its doomed occupants heading rapidly sunward, the spaceship swerved and headed back for Dlasitap.

Kamunioleten was glad to regain his old prestige and position once more on Dlasitap, yet he declined the offer of the Zoromes to make him like his fellow Administrators.

"Let them rule always," he said, "and let my place be filled from time to time."

The five machine men of Dlasitap were found better content to live an endless life on their own world than to rove among the stars with the Zoromes.

After a brief stay on Dlasitap and Selimemigre, the spaceship of the Zoromes once more sped away on its argosy of cosmic adventures, leaving behind two dwindling points of light, one brighter than the other, yet both of which soon disappeared from sight, lost in the distance of interstellar darkness.

ON THE PLANET FRAGMENT

I

THERE IT LAY, slowly gyrating through space, its ponderous and rough-cut, jagged mountain peaks piercing far above the low-lying atmosphere into the endless abyss of space through which the planet plunged. This was the first impression the machine men of Zor had of this strangely shaped world. From afar, they had recognized a departure from the general rotundity characteristic of the major cosmic bodies.

It might have resembled an elongated cube, had not one end been imperfect and receding, so nearly square were the angles of this strange world. Professor Jameson estimated the length of the immense body to vary in the neighborhood of twenty-three thousand miles. As the spaceship sped closer, and the planet turned upon an axis yet to be defined, the cubic illusion grew less, for the planet appeared more like a mighty stone slab, fourteen thousand miles across and four thousand miles thick. Not until the planet had turned slowly around were these figures available. Distantly, the great world had gleamed as an oblate spheroid, but up closer the softening curves induced by reflected sunlight yielded to squarer cut reality.

To have said that it was a flat world would have been voicing no deviation from actual proportions. It was a flat world, its edges four thousand miles thick. The atmosphere appeared unequally divided over the faceted surface. More air apparently enveloped the flat surfaces than covered the sides and ends, especially the ends, which possessed but a thin, scanty layer. The imperfect end tapered gradually into two of the sides, the atmosphere following the surface in ever widening strata as it left the heavier gravity of the receding end. The machine men were of the opinion that gravity and density were the deciding factors concerning the atmosphere. In quantity, the air was more or less equally divided.

"How might such a queer-shaped world ever come to be?" 454ZQ2 ventured. "It is incredible that such a large, cosmic body should be found in this semblance."

"A reason for it exists somewhere," 744U-21 offered. "There are four other worlds to the system, and none of them are like this. All are spherical. And there is another mismated atmosphere."

"It would seem that this world we are approaching is foreign to the system," 6W-438 observed. "It may have come wandering through space ages ago and was captured by this star."

"The solution appears plausible," the professor agreed. "Yet even if we take for granted that it possessed an atmosphere when it reached this system, why does it possess such a queer shape?"

"A cosmic explosion somewhere far off in the universe may have sent it upon its journey," 41C-98 theorized. "The cause we may never know. At least, we can guess at it. As for atmosphere, we have found before that transformed worlds often generate their own during a passing phase of development or reconstruction. A new sun accounts for much."

The conjectures among the machine men were many.

"Two stars passing close to each other may have become wrenched asunder. This great fragment, perhaps, is one of the pieces."

"But the rotating, molten mass would assume a spherical shape."

"Not if the stars, or at least one of them, were cooled and dying."

"A giant planet may have exploded."

"A collision of worlds."

"The fragment cannot be originally from this system. It came from no one knows how far and brought its atmospheric constituents along."

"It seems the only planet of this group on which we might expect to find organisms."

The spaceship described a semi-arc about the huge fragment, and another startling discovery was made. There was a moon, a rough, jagged specimen fifty-five thousand miles distant. The professor estimated its diameter to be less than nine hundred of his Earthly units of measurement. Here again was the departure from the conventional, spherical form, yet strange as it might seem this little satellite conformed more to the shape of a globe than did its mighty companion. But the rough surface with its jagged spires and upflung escarpments was synonomous with the general

67

appearance of its huge contemporary, though it lacked the elongated contour.

As the spaceship sped downward to less than ten thousand miles over the sunlit surface, the Zoromes marveled at the gigantic mountain ranges which reached up out of the atmosphere and into space. They were easily ten to fifteen times as high as any mountains Professor Jameson could recollect on his planet Earth. Near their bases, yet miles above the planet's general surface, the mountains were ringed with snow and ice, or at least what the machine men took for such.

Where the sunlight struck their sides in the realm of the atmosphere, the mountains were weathered and slightly softened in contour, in contrast to the higher portions far above where unveiled sunlight struck dazzling and unsuffused, the shadows sharply etched and as black as the surrounding space.

"If creatures of any kind do live there, how do they ever get across those mountains?" 119M-5 soliloquized moodily.

"They don't," stated 12W-62 positively, "unless they possess spaceships."

"Spaceships is right," said 744U-21. "Airships would do no good there."

"Perhaps they do have spaceships," 141L-14 suggested.

"Raise your anticipations as high as you will," 6W-438 broke in, "But we are scarcely close enough to discover if there are creatures upon this planet, not to mention creatures of the intelligence you have conjured."

"It will be interesting," Professor Jameson stated, "to walk off the edge of the flat world and down its side."

Twice the spaceship circled the huge fragment. They finally cruised low over one of the more sharply defined edges where massive mountains towered a few miles from the world's edge, planning to land here at least temporarily. But if the world's edge proved a lure, what they saw on closer inspection proved even more so. Midway between the mountains and the rim lay a city.

"It is inhabited!" cried 47X-09 from his position at a telescope.

Strange things moved about below them. It was a city, a vast assemblage of rambling, single-storied huts both large and small. Toward the center of the city there rose several more elaborate pieces of architecture.

"The city is walled about!" 6W-438 discovered. "A very high wall surrounds it!"

20R-645 brought the ship rapidly downward, selecting an open spot not far from the central buildings as a landing place. The spaceship came to rest, but where there had been a teeming city now rested silence and apparent desertion. Every one of the inhabitants had scurried out of sight. A vague mental unrest manifested itself to the keen perceptions of the Zoromes.

"They fear us," said 744U-21. "Be ready to act in case of a hostile demonstration."

"They do not seem to be far enough advanced to represent a menace to us," observed 8L-404.

"Not scientifically, perhaps," 744U-21 countered, "yet remember the ohbs—and then on the previous expedition the Emkls of the blue dimension on the planet of the double sun took frightful toll of our ranks. It has been clearly proved to us that various forms of animation possess natural offensives to which we are not wholly invulnerable."

"It might be best," the professor advised, "to preserve as friendly an attitude as possible until they overcome their fear. We must impress upon them mentally that we mean them no harm."

"What a high wall," marveled 41C-98. "It is easily sixty feet high."

"And probably half as thick," added 29G-75. "Why do you suppose they built it?"

"A wall is usually meant to keep something inside or else outside. Being around a city, I should say that it is to keep something out."

"The something must be a colossus to require a wall as large as that one."

"Not necessarily. It may require special height to keep out a type of creature whose natural facilities enable it to jump high."

"Or the menace may carry means of climbing or otherwise elevating itself," 6W-438 reminded them. "744U-21's allusion to the Emkls on the planet of the double sun just put me in mind of the fuzzy stilt walkers."

The professor's attention became riveted upon the surrounding buildings. The houses, or huts, were crude in design, low and rambling. They were made of something resembling cement, and nowhere did they possess a corner, edge or sharp protuberance. Their general appearance was either oblong, spherical or mushroom, and none of them rose

69

to more than twenty feet in height. The apertures were strangest of all. They were oblate, running horizontally in haphazard order. Each domicile possessed three or more of these means of entrance. The average uniformity of these openings was three feet by one foot wide, giving the machine men a rough perception as to the size of the inhabitants.

Many of the apertures were covered on the inside with shutters. Several of them were open, and from time to time the professor caught furtive glances turned momentarily in the direction of the spaceship. The larger buildings were more massive and seemed built of a varying grade of cement, different in shade and texture than that of the more humble habitations clustered below and stretching away on every side to meet the towering walls. Professor Jameson saw that these larger buildings were more perfectly done, and the weathering on their rough sides suggested that they were much older than the lesser buildings about their base. They were more inclined to square proportions, too, although here the corners and sides were rounded and there was the usual lack of spires or other points. The openings were placed in orderly rows and were more uniform in size though of the same oblate shape as in the smaller houses.

Most of the machine men came out of their spaceship and wandered about in the nearby vicinity but were never out of sight of the ship and their comrades, nor did they attempt seeking out the hidden inhabitants of the strange city. The mountains rose out of sight to one side of the city, their base fringed with vegetation, snow taking its place further up, while into space they towered gaunt and bare. To the other side of the city a verdured plain swept away for several miles to end at what looked like the shores of a calm, placid ocean. And indeed it was an ocean, but not of water: an ocean of atmosphere dropped away to a depth of four thousand miles. Looking straight away or overhead, the machine men knew that not more than thirty miles of air kept the massive fragment from being a lifeless world.

The machine men wondered about the city's inhabitants. Professor Jameson wondered moreover what it would be like to walk to the edge of the world and look off into the abyss beyond.

"Night will soon be upon us," said 744U-21, pointing up to the sunlit peaks and then waving a tentacle at the amber sun upon the horizon. "Tomorrow we may know more

70

about the city and its inhabitants. If they do not overcome their fears by then, we shall have to make overtures of friendship to them. It is probable that when morning comes, their timidity shall have been dispersed by our having made no hostile moves during the night. It is clear that they have cause to fear something, for the great wall testifies to that."

The sun disappeared beyond the world's rim, and the unusually long duration of dusk surprised the machine men, for absolute night did not come until the sun had gone beyond the next rim and its rays no longer shone crosswise up into the square angle strata of atmosphere adjacent to the walled city. The long, drawn-out dusk finally yielded reluctantly to the night, and in the blackness occasional sounds appraised the cosmic wanderers that the city's inhabitants were prowling about under cover of darkness. In the clear, fiery starlight, the machine men now and then saw one of their dim, skulking forms. They never came close. A few times, queer, excited cries were uttered.

The night had grown long when a weird, wailing bedlam arose from a distant quarter of the city. Dim, ghastly lights bobbed uncertainly around the city in the direction of the tumult. The machine men saw globes of light sailing and darting about over the huts. The wailing lamentation grew in volume. In the yells, the Zoromes detected warning, fear, bewilderment and despair.

"Something is going on over there not in accordance with the usual city routine," said 6W-438. "We had better investigate."

The suggestion was acted upon, and a party of Zoromes left immediately for the area of tumult and pale brilliance. Running in the direction of the light, they turned down a twisting, irregular avenue between groups of the small huts, breaking suddenly into direct view of the pulsing, changing radiance. The light emanated from the illuminated globes which floated above the huts and darted against the apertures, most of these being closed.

The globes were animate; the professor recognized this at once. And from the wails emerging out of the nearer huts, he realized also that these lighted things were a feared enemy of the inmates. Closer examination of the flying creatures produced the startling discovery that they possessed no wings. Furthermore, their spherical contour was but the illusion of the surrounding brilliance they exuded. Their nucleus might have been globular, but that was more or less

71

indeterminate because of the surrounding spines which grew in every direction, closeby set, giving them a diameter of a yard or more. A slight weaving motion of these spines caused the professor to alter his opinion. They were not spines; they were small tentacles. In fact, these numberless, slim tentacles were the only outward appearance of these creatures. How they maintained their flight was questionable.

Meanwhile, the wailing from inside the huts was rudely punctuated by a startled shriek of agony, a maddening scream of terror and pain. Out of an aperture came one of the flying monsters dragging with it an equally monstrous creature a bit smaller than itself. For the first time, the machine men saw one of the city's inhabitants. Its body was somewhat like a solid wheel, a bewildering set of appendages circling the rim. Toward the center its body broadened slightly. Large optics, one on each side of the disk, were at present distended with terror, while the short appendages, hooked and clawed at their extremities, kicked and fought to tear loose from the curled tentacles which gripped so tightly.

Out of the hut's oblong windows rushed three more of the strange inhabitants, leaping up and setting upon the blazing terror in an attempt to free their helpless companion. With panic written upon their minds, the professor could not help trying to rescue their comrade from the clutches of the marauder. This thought was uppermost in the metal encased heads of all the machine men, and they acted simultaneously as the disengaged monsters of the air raced down upon the howling creatures below them. One of the glowing spheres set its fiery tentacles upon 60M-64 and was promptly torn to shreds, the innumerable tentacles stripped from a tough, pulpy center which was soon ripped to pieces in its own liquid welter.

Meanwhile, the rest of the machine men hurried to the aid of the Disci. The professor leaped upward off the ground and seized one of the shining things just as it slowly rose with a screaming, struggling victim. Bringing the luminous creature down, he found it necessary to tear the malign menace into lifeless sections before it would loose its quarry. There were scarcely a dozen of the things, yet in the confusion and their flying around there seemed more of them. They had immediately seized the luckless creatures who had emerged from the protection of their hut, and one of them was making good an escape, rising above the reach of the machine men who leaped high but to no avail. The victim's despairing screams grew fainter, and the globe of light dwindled.

"If we only had the mechanical wings here!" 6W-438 lamented.

The machine men had killed several of the shining things which flew without wings. They had rescued all the inhabitants of the hut except the one which had been borne aloft out of their reach, and now the remaining raiders arose to join their escaped myrmidon and his quarry. The huts grew dim, and darkness replaced the strange brilliance of the fleeing globes.

The Zoromes illuminated the scene of recent conflict with their body lights, and as they did so the frightened and stupified citizens scrambled inside their dwelling as if from some new horror.

"Shall we go back to the ship for our mechanical wings and pursue the shining things?" queried 53S-7, staring up from the apex of his head at the tiny, disappearing points of light which continued their rise steadily upward.

"There is no use to it," the professor replied. "Let us wait until dawn when we may perhaps gain the friendship of these Disci and learn more about the night's affair."

It was even as they had hoped. The dawning of a new day dispelled the horrors of the night before, and in the daylight, which streamed up over the mountain tops and later down into the walled city as the sun rose higher, the citizens emerged in timorous curiosity, their fear still evident though partly restrained. In their minds, the machine men perceived a leaning toward trustfulness, and they fanned this with reassurance and allusion to their aid of the previous night.

Like concave disks, the city's inhabitants dropped from their strange entrances upon an endless row of appendages. Sometimes they walked with their bodies flat above the ground; then again their movement often characterized the rolling motion like that of a cartwheel. On each side of their disk a large eye peered fearfully at the machine men who found them quite intelligent although their city did not suggest any very large amount of culture or scientific attainment. They were soon persuaded to abandon their soft, smoothly-flowing sounds in trying to make themselves understood in answer to the unmistakable questions radiated upon their minds by the concentrated efforts of the Zoromes. A bit hazy and disjointed were the replies, but the thoughts

73

of the Disci, as the professor had immediately dubbed them for want of a better appellation of reference, were definable, and the Zoromes learned more about the shining things from out of the air, which information, however, was but little.

II

"THEY ARE THE EIUKS!" the machine men were told, the descriptive sound issuing excitedly from one of the eight quivering mouths in the side of a Disc. "they always come by night—never by day!"

"And why not by day?"

"We do not know."

"Perhaps they come in the daytime but you cannot see them because their brilliance is not distinguishable by day," the professor suggested.

"No," the spokesman said, wagging his headless body oddly as he replied. "If they came by day, they would seize us and carry us off as they do by night."

"Evidently they are entirely nocturnal," 6W-438 remarked to his metal companions.

The Oaos come by day as well as by night," one of the Disci ventured, "but they never harm us, and often they combat the Eiuks."

"Who are the Oaos?" the professor inquired.

"They look much like the Eiuks. They are spherical, but they have no arms. In the night they do not shine."

"They come by day?" 744U-21 queried. "That is strange. The Eiuks come at night only."

"Oaos come by day and night both," the machine men were reminded.

"Then what good is your high wall around the city if these things can fly and enter your city at will?" asked 6W-438.

"Oh, the wall is to keep us safe from a danger worse than the Eiuks. The Ooaurs from the land of Exhaustion would kill and devour us and destroy our city if they could. They come and pound at our city wall until often it trembles, and we tremble too—in fear."

"Do the Ooaurs come by day or by night?"

"They come any time, but we are thankful that they do not come very often. It has been a long time since they have been here to the city of Ui. The Ooaurs vary in color and size, and their strength is tremendous. They fight among themselves a great deal, for violence and combat of some kind is their chief amusement."

"And they come from the Land of Exhaustion? Why do you call it that? Where is it?"

"It is on the other side of the hill."

The Disci creature pointed in the direction of the world's edge much to the surprise of the machine men who thought his reference to a hill lay in the direction of the mountains.

"But there is no hill that way," 744U-21 remonstrated to the surrounding Disci. "The world drops off there."

Professor Jameson allowed himself a bit of inward amusement, a condition never experienced by his metal comrades.

"That is what they told Columbus," he remarked to 744U-21. "You see, these Disci have never seen their world from afar, always having lived upon it, and they are not aware that it has an edge. To them, the divide is but the crest of a hill. They can walk on either side, you know."

"Of course," 744U-21 agreed. "And the reason they describe the other side as the Land of Exhaustion is because of its greater gravitational attraction. Fourteen thousand miles is the dimensional diameter in the Land of Exhaustion, while here it is but four thousand miles."

The truth of 744U-21's assertions were proved by further questions asked of the Disci.

"We cannot walk very far beyond the crest of the hill," the machine men were told, "for we become terribly heavy and get out of breath. We have to lay down and rest often. If we go too far, we cannot get back, and we lay down and die."

One of the Disci gave a lurid account of his experience in the Land of Exhaustion. He had fallen exhausted several times returning to his own side of the hill. He had gone too far. The last time he fell he could not rise, and though the top of the hill lay near at hand with relief and recovery beyond, he could not get up and make it, and finally he could not move. His body had grown numb and he was dying when companions from Ui coming to peer over the edge of the hill had rushed down and rescued him.

"There is little to be wondered at that the creatures who live in the Land of Exhaustion are so strong. It is well that you do have strong walls."

"And necessarily high, too. The monsters from the other side of the hill can leap to amazing heights."

"Which is quite credible, too," 6W-438 observed.

"Tell us," urged 744U-21. "Do the Eiuks ever venture into the Land of Exhaustion?"

"Yes—they have, but such occasions are rare. When they did, they were unable to rise again. This, of course, was at night, for the Eiuks never come in the daytime. Our watchers peering over the hill watched them."

"Did they die of exhaustion?"

"No, and it proves that they are stronger than we, for as soon as daylight came they gathered their strength and rose up into the sky and out of sight, even as they do at night after having raided our city."

"Strange and inexplicable," mused Professor Jameson. "We must learn more about the Eiuks from first-hand experience."

"What of the Oaos?" asked 744U-21. "Have they ever entered the Land of Exhaustion?"

"Yes, we have also seen them there. Once they halted a charge of the Ooaurs against our city and chased them far back into their own land. We watched from the hilltop after they had been put to rout."

"And the Oaos were not tired and could rise?"

"We saw them, of course, in the daytime, but we have it handed down from our ancestors that the Oaos are stronger than the Eiuks and can rise out of the Land of Exhaustion anytime, either night or day."

"I fail to see where there is any difference in gravitation either by night or day," said 41C-98.

"The riddle is probably in the mode of flying employed by the Eiuks and the Oaos," the professor replied. "There are indeed many things to be explained here."

On asking where the Oaos and Euks lived, the Disci answered briefly with a significant gesture and upward rolling of large, staring eyes in the direction of the lofty, towering mountain peaks.

"Up there."

The Disci were curious about the machine men, and though failing to fully understand their mechanical construction and its relation to their organic brains, they quite surprised the machine men by somewhat grasping the explanations regarding the spaceship and the existence of other worlds among the glittering stars. It was unusual for a species no further advanced than the Disci to understand, not to mention believing or being able to conceive of such things. This was but still another of the puzzles confronting the machine men of Zor upon the planet fragment.

They debated the question of whether they should rise

on their mechanical wings and search among the mountains for the lair of the shining, tentacled Eiuks or wait for them to raid the city again.

6W-438 was eager for exploring a deep, dark cavern in the mountainside which the Disci, who, they now discovered, called themselves the Uum, shunned through superstitious fear. They claimed it to be the pit of the damned and would not venture near it, let alone explore it. Their antipathy toward it was a strange one, possibly inherited, the machine men deduced, along with their many legends.

At this point, the professor discovered their belief in an afterlife. The Uum claimed that long ago in the age-old past many of their number had been destroyed in the cavern, and that the anguished souls of those who had died still haunted the place, ready to waylay and gather to them the souls of those who entered, to add to their miserable company in the dark, gloomy depths of the mountain.

On the other hand, the Uum believed that after death and subsequent cremation on their funeral pyres, they would go upon the wings of the smoke to an eternity with their ancestors on the other side of the mountain. Around this strange legend there abounded the belief that in the beginning the Uum had dwelt beyond the mountains in luxury and ease, but that they had done something wrong, or some fearful catastrophy had driven them out of his veritable Eden and forced them to live among the constant dangers of the Ooaurs and Eiuks in the walled city of Ui which their ancestors had built. On this last portion of the legend, they were uncertain and hazy.

The Zoromes decided on both searching among the mountains for the Eiuks and exploring the dreaded cavern of the Uum at the same time, dividing their forces into three contingents; the largest body was to remain in Ui with the spaceship. 744U-21 and 41C-98 were to lead a winged party into the towering reaches of the mountain peaks in search of the Eiuks, while the professor and 6W-438 explored the gloomy cave in the mountain along with the remainder of the machine men.

On metal wings, more than a dozen Zoromes rose into the air and headed up the mountain, keeping several hundred feet from the rugged walls and projecting escarpments. The mechanical wings were capable of upholding their possessors in space as well as in atmosphere, for instead of beating the air they employed a repulsion power against gravity.

Meanwhile, before the professor and his metal cohorts

lay the unknown mysteries of the forbidden cavern. A cursory examination of its orifice just before the machine men had separated on their various errands had revealed a trace of ancient waters.

"This must once have been a subterranean waterway," 6W-438 had observed. "This is where the river came out of the mountain."

"It was very long ago," 744U-21 had said, adjusting upon his conical head the temperature equalizer for possible flight into space. "The condition of the rock over which it once flowed discloses this fact, and it is very hard rock, too."

"The stream must have either originated on the other side of the mountain, or else from high up in the mountains where it may possibly follow the vent of an extinct volcano."

"Perhaps," 6W-438 had enthused, "this is a tunnel which leads through to the other side of the mountain."

"Beware of a labyrinth," had warned 744U-21. "Remember well how we became lost in endless, intersecting tunnels on another world. Do not again enter such a place."

"We shall employ extreme care," the professor had promised.

744U-21 then rose to join his winged companions who had disappeared far above. 21MM392 with seven others of the Zoromes then entered the huge opening and walked into the blackness, shining their body lights ahead and to each side.

The course of the ancient waterway turned and twisted, but the general direction was always the same, the confines narrowing and broadening haphazardly. As they progressed deeper into the mountain, the age-old marks of watery passage became less weathered and more sharply discernible. They were glad to find no diversions from the main channel, though occasionally the tunnel expanded for more than a hundred yards. In these widened portions of their course, the professor sent his metal companions in divided groups to follow the walls until they met at a narrowing of the passage deeper into the heart of the mountain. In this manner, they assured themselves of no division in the passage into which they might confusedly lose themselves on their return. Usually, these broad caverns were characterized by a roof much lower than the rest of the channel, though in no instance did the machine men find the roof of the tunnel low enough to reach with upthrust tentacles.

"These caverns are the result of a lower and broadened stratum of softer rock than the strata above and below," the professor commented. "The dissolution of this stratum was governed largely, however, by the rocks and varying forces of the current."

The walls were both smooth and jutted; that is, the projections were not rough or pointed but were polished and rounded. Occasional boulders and potholes marked the floor of the channel, an absence of small stones being noted except those trapped in the potholes. Nowhere did the machine men perceive any danger either to themselves or to the inhabitants of Ui, and this lent strength to the absurdity of the Uum superstition regarding the cavern's frightfulness conjured within the fearful imagainations of the Disci.

Quite without preliminary warning, the machine men came to the passage's end, or at least they believed so, for they explored the sides and ceiling at this point, as well as the floor, for some radical diversion from the usual gentle meanderings they had found. There was no alternative to the conclusion confronting them: this was the end of the passage. Before them lay an accumulation of rock, loose and boulder-strewn at the edges, hard packed and semi-solid beyond.

"The ceiling here caved in at some time or other and shut this off," was 12W-62 suggestion.

"Do you suppose it closed off the subterranean stream?" queried 377X-80.

"On the contrary," 119M-5 interjected. "No cave-in would have halted a stream of sufficient potency to have carved its course out of solid rock. The cave-in occurred long after the river had died away and this channel became dry."

"Suppose the river had dwindled to a small stream," countered 377X-80 for the sake of argument.

"The cave-in evidently occurred long after the stream became extinct," said 6W-438, "for the condition of the fallen ceiling debris does not correspond with the great age of the geological markings made on the walls of this channel by the rushing waters."

"And here is something to lend fact to your theory, 6W-438," the professor remarked, pointing to several small white objects clustered and half buried amid the fallen rock.

"These also give some credence to the superstitions of the Uum."

6W-438 picked up one of the white objects, which crumbled to dust in his tentacles.

"Once these were bones."

"What would you say as to their age?"

"That is a matter for conjecture. A great deal depends upon the atmosphere and climatic conditions on this world, especially in this section; also the conditions in this tunnel, 21MM392."

"I would venture several thousand of my Earthly years," said the professor.

"Then there is something to the legend of the Uum after all?"

"Concerning the destroyed people, yes. The bones prove, or at least suggest, that, but as to the menacing spirits of these dead I believe the Uum have elaborated somewhat."

"There is nothing to do but for us to return," said 6W-438. "We have seen what there was to be found."

The machine men retraced their way, and on quitting the cavern and entering the walled city they found that 744U-21 and his flying Zoromes had not yet flown down from the mountain peaks. They returned that night, reporting that nothing could be found of the Eiuks, but endless ranges to either side of the great valley beyond the nearer peaks might easily hide them. They had searched the mountains closely all day, and with the dropping of the sun beyond the world's edge they had returned.

The Uum were not surprised to see the professor and his seven metal companions emerge safely from the dreaded cavern, nor were they surprised when they were informed that it was a long tunnel which came to an end several miles into the heart of the mountain. When told of the bones, their beliefs became firmer than ever that malign spirits occupied the tunnel, although the machine men attested to the absence of the latter.

744U-21 and those who had flown aloft equipped with mechanical wings and temperature equalizers told of rugged peaks rising high above the atmosphere. From their lofty summits, the machine men had looked down into the endless ocean of atmosphere and gazed off into the abyss beyond the "hill," so called by the Disci. From the snow line to the rocky ramparts on the borderline of space and air, no living thing had they seen, the landscape as lonely and desolate as that upthrust beyond the ocean of air.

With the sinking of the sun into the haze off the edge of the planet fragment, the Disci composed themselves for another night's rest. Since the coming of the machine men, their nights had been peaceful ones. None of the Eiuks had returned following their disastrous clash with the Zoromes,

80

but according to the Disci the raiders from above came only at sporadic intervals.

The next day, the machine men turned their attention to the Land of Exhaustion where lived the frightful Ooaurs of Uum description. It was decided that the spaceship would accompany a party of Zoromes on foot, flying above to insure them against danger from the unexpected.

III

WITH EIGHTEEN COMRADES, Professor Jameson marched in the direction of the world's edge. A bit of eagerness for the moment when he should step off possessed him. He knew he would not fall four thousand miles down the sheer side of the great fragment off into a sea of atmosphere and out into space, yet on approach there seemed to him the prospective illusion of doing so.

The spaceship sailing some hundred feet or more above them neared the rim. Behind the Zoromes, a multitude of the Uum shrilled and squeaked excitedly. Though he knew better, the professor almost expected to stand on the edge of a dizzying depth of precipice, yielding himself momentarily to the illusion. Instead, there came a subtle change as he walked to the divide. It was difficult to explain. It was as if he had walked up a hill without the necessity of exertion or without the consciousness of incline. It almost seemed as if the ground had slowly risen with him as he had walked. There he stood—on the top of the hill. Down one endless slope lay the Land of Exhaustion, while from the direction of the gigantic mountain peaks towering nearly overhead the remainder of the machine men and the Disci walked up the hill to join him. Belying the mistaken impression of the nearby mountains, the dwindled walls of Ui lay far behind them like a toy setting of gnome land.

Fearfully, the Uum peered down into the Land of Exhaustion, chattering in awed accents of the fearsome creatures who came out of this territory to pound at the strong walls of Ui and menace their lives.

The spaceship was a half mile ahead of them over a distant fringe of verdure. Professor Jameson and his metal companions started into the Land of Exhaustion, heading to where the spaceship cruised slowly. At first they noticed no difference from their progress made on the other side of the rim, but as they neared the vicinity of the circling ship

81

a subtle change forced itself upon their consciousness. They were becoming heavy-footed. As if on a denser planet, the machine men merely expanded a bit more energy and tramped onward, soon disregarding this increase of gravity after their interior adjustment of energy release. But with the Uum who dared to follow, lagging feet commenced to manifest their inability to proceed faster.

This may have been partly mental, for the Uum knew that slower procedure would conserve their forces longer just as the mountain climber disdains to rush furiously up the slope. The Uum were occasionally mountain climbers, yet the machine men found that the altitude gained had been pitifully small, especially as compared with the enormous heights of the looming peaks. In the mountains, the cold grew successively for each high ascent, and this, coupled with the hopelessness of ever attaining the frowning, impregnable heights, discouraged the Disci from ever discovering what lay up there, much less what lay beyond.

They were an imprisoned people, hemmed in by mountains which spread away interminably in one direction, while in the distance the mountains first paralleled, then converged with and entered the Land of Exhaustion. In but one direction did the Uum possess free access, and the machine men were already aware that in this direction deep, rugged canyons cut from the mountains into the Land of Exhaustion, and this latter country mockingly represented an avenue of death. If the Ooaurs did not get them, exhaustion did. Thus, the intrepidity displayed by those who followed the machine men into the forbidden land can well be appreciated. They straggled far in the rear of the metal vanguard, often stopping to rest, though this latter respite was scarcely the relaxation they might have expected on their own soil.

At the spot amid some denser vegetation where the spaceship had designated something worth investigating, the machine men found several mounds of white bones, large bones which suggested gargantuan creatures.

"Ooaurs!"

"Presumably. They probably died in combat. The Uum claim that they fight with each other quite often."

"I would say that they were of varying species by the contrasting sizes and formations of their bones."

While the machine men wandered over a large extent of territory, the Uum who had accompanied them turned back to their own land, arriving there tired out. A few of them had difficulty in returning and gained the divide only through the help of fresh companions, waiting at the rim ready to rush forth and help them back again.

The machine men found none of the Ooaurs. In fact, had it not been for the bones, they might have doubted their existence at all, regarding them as figments of Uum imagination, which they were coming to look upon as rather prolific. It was at the suggestion of 12W-62 that they all took to the spaceship.

On the thus possible deeper penetration into this region of greater gravity, they found living specimens of the Ooaurs quite distant from the rim, all of which was well for the Uum. The machine men found variegated and contrasting species, which the Uum evidently classified under a single indiscriminatory title. The Ooaurs were of a quasi-bestial type, showing a very low form of intelligence. Mostly, they were gigantic, towering fully three times as high as the machine men. Their general characteristic, like the Disci, was having many feet, one species boasting of as many as ten. Unlike the Uum, however, they were permanently stabilized, probably because they possessed anterior heads. They lived for the most part in the forests and brush. The machine men did not land, but from on high they occasionally distinguished evidence purporting the exestence of rudely constructed platforms in the trees, or hovels close to the ground. They did not live separately but clanned together in tribes.

Their bodies were lean and angular, yet nonetheless suggestive of brute strength. Four jointed arms ended in barbed claws at the extremities of long, supple fingers. Hideous, wolfish faces were partly obscured by long, unkempt hair which also crept halfway down their backs in a bristling mane. There were variations of the species. Many possessed less appendages than the others, not able to cover ground so swiftly as did their cousins with more legs. One Ooaur tribe possessed little difference between upper and lower limbs except when they stood erect. Coloring, size, occasional absence of the hairy cape and other details varied to set off peculiar types. The separate communities often conducted wholesale battles. In fact, there were ocasional brawls in a single village, which, when considered, was not surprising.

When the spaceship dropped low, the Ooaurs generally welcomed this closer investigation with raucous, bellowing challenges and fearsome gesticulations. At no time did any

83

species seem frightened of the spaceship. The Zoromes disregarded them beyond a cursory examination and sailed on to some other community. At one time, they were on hand to witness a combat between two parties of contrasting Ooaurs. Both sides fought fiercely and without quarter until those surviving represented only one faction. Out of the carnage, the victors ate of their vanquished enemy, slung the remainder across their backs and returned to their village. Their own dead they left behind untouched and unburied.

"Pleasant creatures," 6W-438 observed. "No wonder the Uum have built such a high wall about Ui."

On the cruise back to Ui, the machine men noticed a difference of vegetation from that which they had previously seen at right angles to the Land of Exhaustion. Upon the planetary side of greater gravity similar species varied in growth, showing the altering tendency of gravity, while specimens of plant life seen in the neighborhood of Ui were not to be found at all on that side of the rim.

A tribe of Ooaurs tried to follow the course of the spaceship along the ground but were soon lost from view, and no more of the formidable brutes were seen on the way back to the rim.

Several days passed, and the machine men learned more about the Uum and the vicinity in which they resided. Once, there had been many small communities of the Uum, but the raids of the Eiuks and Ooaurs, so legend had told them, had reduced the Disci to their present numbers and forced them to seek the refuge of a strong, central city. The wandering Zoromes found the remnants of old villages scattered along the world's rim. Running in one direction, the rim merged into the great mountains which flung their lofty parapets over the edge of the huge fragment, while in the other direction the rim became less sharply defined, the edge rounded, flattened and serrated with canyons. At this point it was difficult to define one's position as on either side of the world. In comparison to the enormous bulk of the planet, this tiny facet represented nearly a hundred miles of uncertainty to the wanderer upon its surface. Strangest of all was the river which flowed over the edge of the world. The machine men discovered this beyond the region of the canyons, a river inaccessible to the Uum. The main difference evidenced by its change of location after flowing over the rim into the Land of Exhaustion was the deeper channel it dug, although the depth of water was no more or less, generally. Floating objects possessed less buoyancy too.

The machine men had looked for the Euiks and the Oaos in vain, for they had not found the slightest evidence of them in their search among the mountains. Having witnessed startling proof of the Eiuks, they nevertheless still doubted the existence of the Oaos. The latter, it was understood, though resembling the Eiuks in spherical contour, seemed benevolently disposed to the Uum and were more rarely seen. Both comparison and contrast merged into one. The Uum possessed strange legends, the machine men already knew.

Finally, the event for which they had waited so patiently and expectantly occurred. The glowing Eiuks descended one night upon a raid. A watch of the machine men first discovered them as tiny points of light sinking tranquilly, yet with sinister intent, like slowly detached stars from out of the studded heavens. The alarm was spread among the machine men who donned their mechanical wings in readiness.

"Do not kill unless it is necessary," the professor warned. "We must follow them back to their lair."

The city remained quiet, the Uum unaware of the creeping death from above. Only the machine men knew. There were more than twenty of the tentacled spheres this time, all white and glowing, ready for a raid upon the unsuspecting Disci. Patiently, twenty-three Zoromes waited until the shining globes were just above the city, slowing their descent. For rapid emergency, the machine men carried their deadly ray ejectors; the professor's own weapon was ever ready, permanently installed in a foretentacle. When the first Eiuk dropped to a window the professor gave his signal, and into the horde of descending creatures the machine men swooped, circling the scintillating globes.

Apparently unafraid, the Eiuks became only mildly surprised, perhaps momentarily disconcerted. Fearlessly, they sprang to attack this flying interruption of their intended feast. They were met with grinding coils of metal and deadly rays which matched their own peculiar brilliance, killing and maiming to right and left. So silent was the attack and its deadly counter thrust that the inhabitants of the city slept on, blissfully ignorant of the carnage so close above them. They might have remained unknowing until morning had not a falling Eiuk, its corpse devoid of all fiery life, struck the roof of a dwelling with considerable

85

noise, arousing the inmates. Startled Disci ogled their huge eyes at the confused swarm of Eiuks, around which the flying Zoromes were twisting and turning in flight.

A screech of alarm in turn aroused the sleeping Uum in the surrounding buildings until the din was such as it had been on that night when the machine men had first encountered the brilliant, spiny spheres from above. Let it be said, however, that in accordance with the immediate telepathic instructions of the circling Zoromes, the Disci did not emerge from their homes, and they kept the entrances closed.

Baffled, defeated and reduced in numbers, the Eiuks abandoned their attack on the city of Ui and slowly rose into the sky. Those who still lived left the scene of their defeat like lifted lamps, unhurried and majestic, unhurried because the machine men did not feel prone to accelerate their departure, majestic because their flight was directly vertical like the ascent of a balloon in still air. Where more than twenty of the shining balls had dropped into the walled city, only eight glowing orbs ascended, and beneath these the machine men of Zor slowly rose in passive pursuit.

"Where are they from?"

Each Zorome pondered the question, and the suggestions were many.

"The mountains."

"Above or below the atmosphere?"

"Above—in space."

"What? On the frozen, desolate peaks where they cannot breathe?"

"Why not?" 6W-438 asked. "Did not the creatures of the outer crust on the sunless world exist without respiration?"

"But these things can only ascend where there is air upon which to ascend."

"That is more or less to be taken for granted," the professor interposed. "We do not know for a certainty. Our mechanical wings are capable of carrying us into space."

"To be sure," said 119M-5. "We carry repulsion charges, but what is their mode of ascent?"

No one of them yet knew. They could only resort to conjecture once more.

"They live beyond the mountains."

"Then they possess acclimation and movement in space in order to cross over them."

"It is more likely that they live in the mountains below

the air limit," offered 6W-438. "There may be a defile somewhere, giving them access beyond the peaks, seeing that we have searched on this side of the range and have failed to find them."

The Eiuks rose in a straight line until air currents swept them closer to the towering mountains, yet they did not land but continued to rise. The machine men followed but made no manifestations of their pursuit. Whether or not the Eiuks possessed knowledge of their being followed the machine men did not know. What little intelligence the shining bodies held remained imperceptible to the mental probings of the Zoromes.

The drifting globes finally ceased to rise, floating along on a current of air straight for the dark, somber mountainside. They were far up in the rarified atmosphere. Approaching closer to the mountains, the machine men distinguished uncountable multitudes of the shining spheres either at rest on the ground or else slowly bobbing up and down like rubber balls under low gravitational attraction.

"We searched this section of the mountains very carefully!" one of the machine men exclaimed. "Nowhere did we find even a trace of the Eiuks!"

"They may not have been here at that time, especially if they are migratory," 6W-438 ventured.

"It is also possible that in daylight they are invisible," Professor Jameson suggested.

As far as they could see in every direction, the shining, animate globes dotted the mountains. The machine men soared far above in order to obtain a more composite view. There were literally millions of the things. Like the lights of a long, straggling city, they stretched away into the distance until black peaks and rugged escarpments blotted them from sight. One peculiarity, however, struck the machine men as significant. The Eiuks seemed generally confined to a definite strata of altitude. There were a scattered few who shone upon lower levels, but above the main, glowing band that stretched away over the rugged slopes, all was darkness. Below this darkness, the bobbing lights, fewer among their more stationary brethren, made a curious, changing pattern.

"We shall wait and see if they disappear and become invisible in the daytime," Professor Jameson said. "We must know more about them."

They had not very long to wait for dawn, and soon after came daylight, yet sunlight lagged much longer due to the immense heights to which the mountain range penetrated. Dawn had first shown its fingers from the direction of the far-off canyon. The machine men watched the Eiuks closely with the coming of dawn. At the first lessening of darkness, a curious unrest became noticeable among the shining spheres. Looking down from positions far up on the side of a towering cliff, the machine men saw the entire assemblage of Eiuks commence to bob up and down. This strange motion became more pronounced until suddenly several out of each hundred or more commenced to rise slowly. With the increase of light, more of them followed in that majestic, stately rise which was so characteristic of them. Their brilliant glow became less noticeable as dawn merged into daylight, and they rose like slow bubbles in a heavy liquid.

With the coming of daylight, an awesome panorama of terrifying splendor thurst itself upon the mechanical vision of the Zoromes. So high up were they that seemingly at the foot of the peaks lay the awful abyss dropping into the Land of Exhaustion. Like a tiny square below them lay the city of Ui, while all about in colossal grandeur rose the mighty peaks, visible far up beyond the atmosphere only where the unveiled sunlight glared dazzling from their towering pinnaces.

Like burnished, bronze bubbles, the Eiuks rose in a steady stream ever skyward. They reached the level of the waiting Zoromes and still they continued to ascend, gaining momentum as the daylight waxed brighter.

"Follow," was Professor Jameson's one thought.

And the mechanical-winged Zoromes, releasing their holds and positions among the niches and narrow ledges of the precipices, followed the upward flight of the Eiuks. No longer were they the shining, glorious objects of nightfall. Daylight had outrivaled their nocturnal splendors, reducing them to the orange balls they appeared to be. The machine men kept close to the mountains; the Eiuks kept going straight up, not pausing to rest on the higher altitudes they were passing. Occasionally, below them, an Eiuk would cling with tentacles to either a rough bit of rock or sparse vegetation. The creatures were pulled as with an invisible hand toward their rising companions; the vegetation then came away and the clinging Eiuks shot up more rapidly then their fellows. One, clinging to a rock, sluggishly carried the rock up with him.

"I have an idea," said the professor.

"What is it, 21MM392?" 6W-438 inquired.

SHOOTING THROUGH the air, the professor headed straight among the Eiuks who sprang away from him a bit, yet never ceased their upward course. The professor interwove a curling tentacle among the numerous tentacles of an Eiuk. Quickly he seized another of the creatures and still another, clinging tightly to all three. Releasing his power of repulsion, he felt his dead weight hang on the struggling Eiuks. Their ascent slowed to a standstill; then they commenced to drop slowly. The professor took the opportunity to examine his three live captives and nowhere could he discover any methods of flight. He only saw that the many tentacles of the things seemed harder than those of the dead creatures the machine men had previously examined on coming to the city of Ui.

The rest of the Zoromes circled among the rising multitudes of Eiuks, confident that there was no longer any danger of frightening them from seeking their habitual haunts. They seemed unable to resist a strange, compelling call which drew them ever upward.

Slowly but steadily, the three Eiuks to which Professor Jameson resolutely clung dropped in reluctant descent. The machine man could feel and sense some power which attracted them from above. Then that for which he had looked occurred: in a blaze of glory, a penetrating beam of light shot out from between two peaks and grew broader and brighter as the sun burst into view. The professor realized a subtle change. Their drop became slower, and finally they barely moved. The first thing he knew they were rising again. A few laggard Eiuks shot past them to join the main van far above. Several machine men hovered in the vicinity of the professor, while the large number of Zoromes flew steadily upward with the Eiuks. The professor released one of the creatures, which shot like a plummet into the rarified atmosphere above. Still their ascent continued, yet noticeably checked. Releasing the remaining tentacles, Professor Jameson allowed the other two Eiuks to join their companion, while he dropped with the speed of a falling object. Checking his accelerating momentum with an application of his mechanical repeller wings, he rose with his metal companions.

"I believe I have cleared up several conjectures in our minds," he said.

"I can anticipate your discoveries," offered 6W-438. "The secret of the phenomenal rise of the Eiuks is due to daylight, sunlight especially."

"Exactly," the professor agreed.

"And their domain in the daytime is the highest reaches of the upper atmosphere, while at night they descend to lower levels. What power to you suppose daylight exerts upon them?"

"I would say that it generates a gas within them which they cannot release fast enough in the daytime to remain on lower levels. At night, they have more control over it. This would allow them to descend to lower levels and raid the Uum. We shall see if they do not rise to the outer limits of the atmosphere much like an object lighter than water rises to the surface of an ocean."

The ascent of the Eiuks became modified, a goodly number of them failing to rise any more. The professor perceived multitudinous fields of the floating, orange globes far above, now at rest on the outskirts of the atmosphere. They could rise no further. From above the edge of the world to the great mountains, their uncountable legions stretched away into waning perspective. Above this galaxy of sentient Eiuks rose the machine men of Zor, the belated professor and his two companions joining them.

"At night," opined the professor, "these creatures will be generating less gas and will drop to lower levels."

"They probably feed on the mountainside," 12W-62 suggested.

"Or on the Uum when they descend that low," 6W-438 added. "Why is it they do not come oftener to Ui? There are such countless numbers of them."

"It is possible," advanced 41C-98, "that only during certain phases of their lives are they able to descend into such dense atmospheric depths, perhaps some physical condition being responsible for it."

"Even as the eels in the oceans of my Earth," mused Professor Jameson, his mind bridging the interminable abyss of time.

"All of which destroys any relationship between the Eiuks and the Oaos we may have theoretically established," 744U-21 reminded his metal companions as they sped swiftly above the bobbing assemblage of sun-tinted spheres. "We have it on word of the Uum that the Oaos have been seen during the daytime. They have also befriended the Uum against the Ooaurs and Eiuks, if these tendencies can be accepted as entirely altruistic."

"I believe the existence of the Oaos to be a myth," affirmed 41C-98. "With all the dangers that beset them, the Uum certainly need a mythical means of hope and moral support."

Such were the divided opinions of the machine men as they penetrated through the suspended ranks of the Eiuks and fell toward Ui in a series of long drops. Back in the walled city they told of their adventures above the stratosphere of the odd-shaped world, how they had found the lair of the shining globes and had solved the mystery of their nocturnal raids. Of the Oaos, however, they had learned nothing. In fact, they knew less about them, for their previous theories had become discarded in the light of the ensuing discoveries. The machine men of Zor tried to learn more about the Oaos from the Disci, but all they could obtain were repetitions of the few scanty details previously told to them.

The next day, several Uum came running and gabbling to the city gate. They had come from the borders of the Land of Exhaustion where a large band of Ooaurs had been sighted. The brutes were heading for the world's edge. In fact, a swift glance from the walls of the city aroused consternation and alarm, for the Ooaurs were to be seen in the distance, coming over the rim.

Machine men suspended repair work on their spaceship, which they had moved to a convenient location within the city walls. All Disci outside the city scurried for the safety of Ui where the huge gates were being hurriedly closed. Comrades were allowing them entrance through small openings which were hastily closed and barred once the Uum had gained sanctuary.

In the distance, halfway between Ui and the rim of the world, a single Disci rolled madly along his endless row of feet like a whirling cartwheel. A mingled roar was emitted from the foraging Ooaurs, and several of them set after him with rapidly increasing speed. It was a desperate run for life, but the finish was soon apparent. The Ooaurs thundered along at a terrific gain, and 284D-167, the machine man who ran futilely to intercept the dreaded creatures, was far too late to be of any help.

Ferociously, the howling, triumphant Ooaurs raced down upon their fleeing quarry in a cloud of dust which partly veiled the vicious and competitive tearing apart of the luckless victim even as the echo of his one piercing shriek rolled back from the massive walls of Ui. Four machine men on vantage points of the protecting wall dropped to the ground and ran to where 284D-167 was now becoming the central object of the approaching Ooaurs, who sensed still another easy victim. All five were unarmed. Of these, 5ZQ-35 sent back a mental admonition to the machine men within the walls.

"Bring ray ejectors! Their numbers are many!"

While three of the Ooaurs hastily bolted down the remains of the Uum they had so easily caught, at least six of the huge creatures descended in a rush upon 284D-167 who went down beneath their thrashing bodies before the arrival of his hurrying companions. Herculean appendages tugged and tore at his metal parts. In the heat of competition, the Ooaurs were slow to realize that something was materially wrong with this thing they had selected as their prey. Their sluggish minds became first of all surprised, and then they became irritated to exasperation.

Meanwhile, a tentacle had twined itself about a shaggy leg, and under pressure the tortured Ooaur bellowed in threshing pain and rage, blindly belaboring his companions and tugging madly at the metal cube beneath them.

It was at this moment that 5ZQ-35, 7H-88, 168P-75 and 8L-404 rushed to the aid of their fallen comrade. Coming to grips with the gigantic Ooaurs, the machine men realized that there they had no easy adversaries despite their own advantages. Moreover, several more Ooaurs were coming to join the fray in the hopes of obtaining a part of the kill, the rest sweeping on to the walled city.

The combat of the five machine men and their huge adversaries resolved itself into a strange battle of pulling, hauling, squeezing and ineffective biting. 168P-75 and 5ZQ-35 each felt a tentacle pulled from their bodies, while a leg had been bent beneath 284D-167 in the general rush.

Ooaurs were beating and yelling at the walls. Upon each others' backs they climbed, gathering pyramids for ascent. Uum, terrified but resolute, patrolled the walls with long, sharp pikes, ready to stab at the leaping, climbing beasts that came close enough for them to reach. The Ooaurs fell back in howling anguish when stabbed, madly beating the walls with fisted paws. Their ability to leap nearly to the top of the wall was both surprising and appalling. One savage leap resulted in the seizing of a threatening pike, pulling its wielder off the wall and into the anticipatory grasp of several Ooaurs.

These were the sights which met the eye of Professor Jameson and seventeen companions as they sprang up onto the wall with ray ejectors ready. The professor was never without his, for it was built into the extremity of a fore-tentacle. A burning bath sprayed the Ooaurs, quickly turning the raid into a rout. Dead and wounded fell thick beneath the walls before the great brutes realized their danger and fled. The Uum, never having killed an Ooaur or having seen a dead one, marveled at the efficacy of the ray ejectors. To them, the conquest of the Ooaurs was vastly more amazing than the deaths and frustration of the Eiuks. The shining spheres on their night visits evoked a different sort of terror, something akin to supernatural dread. The machine men were such strange and unworldly creatures that it had not seemed so surprising that they should have conquered the Eiuks, but the Ooaurs were more tangible and physically adaptable to their restricted imaginations. The Disci understood the Ooaurs more readily. To the Uum, darkness and mystery lent the Eiuks imaginative terrors.

Most wonderful and more sensational to the sight of the Uum were the individual combats outside of the walls between the five machine men and their adversaries outside of the walls. Outnumbered two to one, crippled but unconquered, the indomitable Zoromes were emerging victorious. The ripping tattoo of metal feet and the crushing power of serpentine tentacles were telling a tale of mastery over flesh and brute strength. In maddened pain, the Ooaurs occasionally flung a machine man into the air and made good their retreat, but most of those who had entered the fight with the machine men were strangled to death, battered to shreds by metal feet or otherwise torn and lacerated into expiring heaps. 5ZQ-35 waged a difficult combat with only one tentacle left. Under the tremendous pressure exerted on his metal legs, 8L-404 could no longer walk; he could only crawl on his bent, lower appendages. But victory was soon theirs.

In the distance, the escaping Ooaurs disappeared rapidly over the world's edge into the Land of Exhaustion, more than a dozen Zoromes pursuing them with the searing, burning death. No time had been taken to don the mechanical wings, and the machine men found the Ooaurs well equal to their pace over the terrain. The machine men found they did not gain on the Ooaurs, but it was their desire to keep pushing them deeper into their usual stamping grounds in order to discourage a further attack upon the walled city of Ui.

Straight into the Land of Exhaustion the machine men followed the retreat of the monsters. Occasionally one fell behind because of some injury sustained in the raid on the Uum. In such instances the laggards were quickly dispatched, and the machine men thrust further on in pursuit, passing the first fringes of vegetation and spreading out widely to prevent even a temporary pause of the Ooaurs.

The professor found himself next to 27E-24, who represented the extreme left flank. The Zoromes had now spread so far apart that the professor was no longer in mental contact with the machine man on his right. With this realization, the professor notified 27E-24, and they both swung to the right, yet kept straight on in a slanting line which would bring them nearer the main body of Zoromes.

27E-24 and the professor pushed their way through a sparsely verdured forestland, possibly a half mile or more from each other, when a mental cry arrested the forward progress of Professor Jameson.

"21MM392! Ooaurs! They are attacking me!"

It was 27E-24, and he had stumbled upon the vicious creatures.

"Use your ray ejector!" The professor advised him. "I am coming!"

"There are many of them—and 21MM392—they are not the ones we were pursuing! They are a different species of Ooaurs!"

The professor ran rapidly in the direction of the fray where 27E-24 was being beset by a large body of the Ooaurs.

"They are too many for me, 21MM392! They know no fear, although I have killed at least three of them and injured more! My ray ejector has been knocked out of my grasp, and they are upon me by weight of numbers!"

Professor Jameson dodged in and out among the bushes and strange giant plants. He came in sight of the Ooaurs who had risen from the overwhelmed machine man and were pulling him away. 27E-24 struggled valiantly, but his burly captors were several times his own size, and he was surrounded, his tentacles held firmly and at a respectful distance from his lower limbs.

Rushing upon them, the professor blazed away with his built-in heat ray. An Ooaur dropped before they were aware of his swift and silent arrival, but once they had seen him they were not slow to act. A quick glance showed him that fully thirty Ooaurs comprised the party, several of them straggling behind in what might have been described as a haphazard rear guard. It was this latter division that wheeled upon him so swiftly and viciously.

The professor knew he would be better off if he kept free from their dexterous clutches of brute strength, especially since they were so overwhelming in numbers; he eluded their charge, therefore, waving his heat ray at them and turning to aid 27E-24 in escaping the many-legged monsters. Simultaneously, 27E-24 put up a herculean struggle; this caused his captors much concern and discomfort but failed its purpose. Professor Jameson had reckoned without consideration of the amazing speed the Ooaurs were capable of exhibiting. While he sprang clear of the first charge, his heat ray burning death among the Ooaurs who held his metal comrade pinioned, the rest of the creatures raced down upon him. Before he knew it, the professor, too, was a prisoner, even though his heat ray had claimed four of the monsters. He continued to blaze a path of havoc among the lower appendages of the brutes until one of them, exerting the power of three mighty arms and snarling horribly, jerked the dangerous foretentacle away from the professor's cube.

Life was cheap here. The Ooaurs paid no attention to their fallen brethren, the dead being left where they had succumbed, the wounded and disabled limping off in the rear of the now triumphant savage company. The necessity that was mother to the act of tearing away the tentacle with its damaging heat rat awakened a sluggish inspiration in the stupid mind of the beast who had performed it. With much growling and chattering, accompanied by obvious pantomine, he finally made it clear to his fellows that they would experience a great deal less trouble and hazardous inconvenience were they to pull away all of the tentacles of the things they had captured.

To the equal consternation of the professor and 27E-24, the Ooaurs put this plan into practice, uniting their energies until the two machine men were without upper appendages. Greedily, several of the monsters tried eating the disengaged tentacles, finally throwing them away in growling disgust. The idea of removing the tentacles furthered the inevitable design of similar removal of the legs. Here the Ooaurs experienced more difficulty, for the metal legs did not come off so easily. They wrenched, bent and

95

twisted until they had succeeded in pulling off five of the metal legs, three from 27E-24 and two from the professor. The machine men were now absolutely helpless, their remaining legs unusable and damaged beyond repair by the tremendous efforts exerted by their captors.

The metal bodies were picked up and carried by two of the Ooaurs, the entire horde heading rapidly deeper into the Land of Exhaustion. From what the machine men could learn from their small brains, the Ooaurs were heading back for their village.

V

"I HOPE THEY do not touch our heads," said 27E-24.

"It is unlikely that they will, unless they should become curious regarding our mechanical eyesight, and even then there is little that they could do."

"I dislike the thoughts of what a well-aimed rock or heavy club wielded by one of these giants might do to our precious heads."

"It is not likely to occur to them." The professor reassured his companion, though he was a bit nervous over their prospects himself. "We can only wait until the spaceship is repaired and they can come in search of us."

"They may come on the mechanical wings."

"It is improbable that those who came with us will find us. We are now headed off on a tangent from the course we originally chose. It was our ill fortune to stray from mental contact with the rest and chance upon this band of Ooaurs different from those we had routed."

The Ooaurs jogged onward. The character of the ground over which they were passing changed. The plain came to an end on this portion of the flat world, and gentle slopes and valleys replaced the level monotony. In one of these valleys lay the village of the Ooaurs. It was dirty and filthy. That was the first impression the machine men gained from the heterogeneous collection of huts and shelters erected from branches, boulders and rock slabs, embellished here and there with a composition of twigs and dried clay. Often, the central stanchions were the trunks of living trees. The architecture spoke not only of ignorance, but laziness as well. Ooaurs rushed out of shelters nearly fallen to pieces through lack of repair as the returned hunting party entered the village, chattering in boastful excitement of the strange things they had captured by pulling off their arms and legs.

The two machine men were dumped unceremoniously on the ground amid the central collection of huts. The setting sun shone dully off the metal bottom of Professor Jameson's cube because he had fallen on one side. 27E-24 had been dropped right side up, slightly tilted toward the professor where a single bent and useless leg upheld him slightly. The two helpless Zoromes became at once the objects of questing, feeling claws as the Ooaurs examined them attentively yet uncomprehendingly.

"Keep your eyes closed," Professor Jameson warned his companion. "We do not want their curiosity to lead them into too prying an examination of our heads."

But like the professor, 27E-24 had also closed his eye shutters soon after entering the village, and if the Ooaurs recollected a difference they did not stress it as of any importance. One of them waved a dangling metal tentacle with voluble explanations concerning its relation to the trophies they had brought back with them. The machine men were tipped and rolled about until the long enduring dusk had finally yielded to darkness. Darkness had long before fallen on Ui and its surrounding country, and the two Zoromes wondered what was happening there. Had their companions returned to Ui from the Land of Exhaustion? Then they were already missed. Or had they finally caught up to the fleeing Ooaurs? If so, they might not have returned this soon.

The dismembered machine men were positive of one condition, however: on their failure to return in proper time, a search would be instituted for them regardless of whether the spaceship was fit to cruise once more or not.

A short night yielded to a steady fringe of light upon the distant horizon which heralded the new day. The village of Ooaurs aroused itself from bestial sleep. The sun crept rapidly over the world's edge, and the new day was born.

Once more the curiosity of the Ooaurs manifested itself in their critical and awkward examination of the machine men's torsos. The professor was once turned and balanced on the apex of his head. The Ooaur released his hold and the heavy cube fell flat upon the feet of another beast. This one howled his pain and smote the careless offender for dropping the body. There came a growling retaliation, and the two ill-tempered monsters were at each other tooth

97

and nail. From his sidewise position, it reminded the professor of a dog fight, with all the other dogs gathering in a circle of acclaiming din and howls. Whatever degree of intelligence they came across, from the greatest to the least, the Zoromes invariably found that creatures of flesh and blood enjoyed watching a fight.

The combat resolved itself into a rough and tumble, biting affair, but its outcome was forever left in doubt. Shrill cries from outside the ring of spectators turned the interested onlookers to a new attraction, one in which they found alarm rather than enjoyment. The audience disappeared, leaving the growling, surging contestants momentarily unaware of the turn events had taken. The battling brutes only stopped fighting when they heard particularly shrill cries—cries unlike any the machine men had yet heard their captors emit. Then their whole demeanor changed and they rose to join their companions, now surging back to the center of the village in a retreating mass.

From the opposite direction, there came a charging horde of Ooaurs, more darkly colored than those the machine men had yet seen. They were more squat, yet none the less bulky, and their hair grew longer. The machine men realized now the consternation of their captors and the cause for alarm. The village was being attacked by a different species of Ooaurs, and the latter species appeared to be in the majority, also brandishing large clubs. Some of them carried as many as four, one in each long-digited claw.

From the slowly retreating mass of villagers, into whose ranks the newcomers suddenly fell, the two helpless Zoromes deduced that superior numbers were pressing them from the front. Attacked on two sides and taken by surprise, the fate of the villagers was already apparent, for the end presaged itself. The carnage and slaughter, most of which was obscured from the stationary view of the two Zoromes by the dark brown, thickly-haired bodies of the invaders, was terrible. The machine men learned this later, when the field of battle had been cleared. The villagers fought to a hopeless finish, though, giving a good account of themselves. Quarter was neither given nor asked.

Not satisfied with what loot and plunder they could find, which strangely enough appeared to consist mainly of odd-shaped bones, the victors engaged in an unrestrained orgy of vandalism. They tore down the homes of their vanquished foes, strewing refuse all over the village and scarcely leaving one stick in orderly contact with another. Others amused themselves by bashing in the heads of any wounded survivors not of their own tribe.

The two machine men were quickly discovered once the villagers had all been dispatched, and once more they underwent first-hand observation and handling. These conquerors had never seen the machine men in action, and so in no way did the two Zoromes give evidence of any sentient character. To the Ooaurs, they were merely ornaments whose acquisition the villagers had in some way managed. The weak concentrative energies of the Ooaurs spent little conjecture on this point. To the victors belonged the spoils, and these marvelous cone-pointed cubes of hard, glistening metal were the greatest prizes of all.

The machine men hoped against any curiosity the Ooaurs might show in regard to their inner contents. Though their metal heads were constructed to withstand severe usage, they feared the consequences of a repeated attack on their heads with the powerfully wielded bludgeons.

Having created all the disorder and destruction of which their poor imaginations were capable, the Ooaurs evacuated the scene of desolation and death, carrying away with them their new acquisitions. Once more the machine men were carried off by Ooaurs, this time in a tangent direction skirting the great plain, a direction promising to bring them gradually closer to the edge of the world. For a long time, the invading warriors held to their course, constantly shifting their weighty burdens in order to keep pace with their fellow creatures.

It was Professor Jameson who first saw the approaching specks on high. A mental flash to 27E-24 appraised him of the professor's initial hope that flying Zoromes had come in search of them, but these hopes became dissipated as the objects in the sky came nearer. That they were bright and reflected the sunlight like the metal sides of a machine man's cube the professor verrified by their closer approach, but they were nothing resembling Zoromes. They were, seemingly, balls of metal.

"Oaos!" exclaimed 27E-24, echoing the thought of the professor. "They do exist! There are three of them!"

"They are coming down here!" the professor exclaimed. "Yes, they are metal, but what are they?"

The metal globes floated nearer so that now the Ooaurs, too, noticed them. In mingled surprise and excitement, they shouted, pointed upward and gesticulated.

"Tiny spaceships—or aircraft," 27E-24 surmised.

"We have seen no creatures here small enough to occupy them," said the professor. "These globes are much smaller than the Eiuks. A single Uum would have difficulty in getting himself into one, regardless of necessary mechanism."

"It is directed by an intelligence. That is apparent. We must communicate with them."

Both machine men sent out strong mental calls, their minds searching for an answer or inkling that they had been heard. Searchingly they sought, and they found only a blank. Yet the three globes still descended, two of them coming close above the heads of the Ooaurs. Above the captive machine men, they paused and kept pace with the captives. The two Zoromes had an excellent opportunity, and they closely examined the metal globes, finding exterior markings suggestive of inner mechanism. In turn, they felt themselves minutely examined. This feeling originated from the actions of the three Oaos rather than a telepathic source, for of the latter there appeared to be no existence.

"Do you suppose they are mechanisms like ourselves, governed by an organic brain?"

"I doubt it," the professor made reply. "If that were so, we would have found it out, yet on the other hand I recall that in the secret city of 6D4 back on the planet of Mumed, his towers were constructed to be thought-proof, so it may be that these globes are made in such a manner."

The Ooaurs were making warlike gesures with their clubs. One of them threw a bludgeon at the lowest of the globes. A shower of upflung missiles followed this initiative, and several clubs clattered and glanced off the bright sphere. Out of the globe shot a glistening stream of green liquid, then another, full upon a cluster of the Ooaurs.

Dense puffs of acrid smoke arose from the doused creatures, who fell screaming in contorting agony. Their companions fell back, choking from the fumes which came from them as their motions and sounds became stilled. They lay dead, yet the smoking vapor still rose, as their inert forms became smoldering, withered, eaten-away semblances of their former selves. The Ooaurs fled them in terror, yet the ire of the Oaos seemed yet unappeased. The two from on high shot several streams of the green death upon the strung-out cavalcade of Ooaurs.

In consternation, the professor saw one of the terrible streams strike close to his metal cube. An Ooaur received it full upon the head, and it spattered on the surrounding

100

beasts and the professor's head and cubed body. Its emerald film obscured the sight of one eye. Puffs of smoke wafted angrily from the stricken Ooaurs and their maddening pain caused the air to resound with agonized shrieks. They ran in aimless circles, beating madly at their bodies and rolling upon the ground. Some ran in a straight line until they fell dead or foaming in terror, their anguished screeches descending in volume like the wail of a departing siren. Others fell upon their companions in pain-crazed rage, enveloped in the fumes of their living cremation. The professor's brain stood still, fastened upon a single, terrifying thought: what would the green liquid do to metal? Nothing happened immediately, and the suspense became partly lifted. . . .

What the liquid was doing to the Ooaurs was vividly and startlingly apparent. They were either dead or dying, all those struck by the liquid, and whether dead or dying the action of the fatal liquid was impartially the same. It ate up its victims swiftly. The remainder of the frightful beasts scattered in aimless flight, impelled by the terror fallen among them. Professor Jameson felt himself dropped with a bump onto one side. He had been abandoned by his carrier, either through a single desire for more speed in escaping the death from on high, or else because of a simple-minded conviction that the mysterious metal things were somehow allied to the flying globes whose material so closely resembled theirs. This latter thought occurred to the professor. His fallen position enabled him to see that 27E-24 had also been delivered a like disposition, the Ooaurs hurrying madly from the scene.

The Oaos seemed no longer interested either in Ooaurs or Zoromes. They had not risen but were slowly drifting away out of the professor's sight—which was largely blocked by his own metal cube, anyway, because he lay on his side. He presently called to 27E-24, who was slightly tilted on one corner.

"Where are the Oaos now?"

"They are leaving, going toward the edge of the world."

"Do they seem bound for Ui?"

"It is probable, though my sense of direction has become rather confused by the character of this flat-sided world."

"The Uum, if their reports are true, have nothing to fear from the Oaos. The Oaos seem friendly to them, though the Uum seldom see them."

"Where do you suppose they come from?"

"The Land of Exhaustion."

101

"We still do not know what they are."

"It is possible that the metal globes are operated by remote control, but logical reasoning would argue against that possibility," the professor stated. "A form of life intelligent enough to build those things would be likely to occupy them as well."

"Do you suppose the Oaos could be from another world of this system—one of the original planets?" 27E-24 queried.

"Possibly, yet it would be more probable that they are from another facet of this strange world. It has six sides, you know, presenting at least three varying forms of environment, two of which we already know."

"The gravity must be tremendous on the two ends," mused 27E-24.

Thus wandered the conversation of the two Zoromes as the day grew clear and they waited in motionless silence at the edge of the vast plain, abandoned and solitary. The fleeing Ooaurs had long ago disappeared; the scurried dust from their many feet had settled. The helpless machine men pondered the question now uppermost in their minds: when would their companions come and find them? And as the day grew in length, so grew the assurance of the professor that the green liquid spattered on him from the metal globe would prove harmless to metal.

The sun hung low, gradually nearing the world's edge, where soon it would sink beyond the sea of atmosphere. It was 27E-24 who first noticed the return of the Oaos in the distance. They were returning from the direction of Ui. The machine men counted them. One-two-three-*four!* There had been but three previously. Now there was another. Four? The professor looked again carefully, for in the distance more dark specks became visible and grew in perspective. They came straight for the lonely, abandoned machine men of Zor. The approaching globes of the Oaos shone in the sky like gibbous moons, reflecting the light of the sinking sun.

It was 27E-24 who first noticed that only three of them presented this gibbous aspect. The rest did not appear as globes. Glimmering suspicion became mother to the confirming truth: only three of the flying things were Oaos. The rest were Zoromes on the wing!

"It can only mean that the Oaos have been to Ui and have brought our machine men back here with them," said the professor. "They have brought them back to find us."

And Professor Jameson was right. His flying companions

were soon about him and 27E-24, while the Oaos hovered far above.

"The spaceship is coming," said 119M-5, pointing to a looming bulk upon the horizon. "What happened, and where do the Oaos figure in this?"

"We were captured by Ooaurs," the professor replied briefly, omitting mention of the fight in the village and how they had involuntarily traded captors. "The Oaos came and frightened away the Ooaurs so that they left us and ran, those whom the Oaos did not kill."

The professor cast mental attention upon the burnt ashes dotting the plain about them.

"But what are the Oaos?" 744U-21 asked. "We cannot communicate with them, despite their intelligent actions."

"You know as much as I do about them," the professor confessed. "The Oaos came and left silently except for their attack upon the Ooaurs with a greenish, burning liquid they are capable of ejecting."

"Do you suppose they are like us?" 41C-98 queried as the spaceship dropped slowly groundward. "Have they organic brains?"

"If they have, they are strangely uncommunicative," 6W-438 observed. "They came to Ui, hovering over the city, arousing the acclaim and excitement of the Disci. After a while, they started slowly for the rim and the Land of Exhaustion; we were preparing to start in search of you and 27E-24, so we followed. They were silent to all our queries."

VI

"THEY ARE FRIENDLY. That is certain."

The two Zoromes were taken aboard the spaceship where their heads were removed and placed upon new cubes already equipped with tentacles and legs. It was found that their original cubes had suffered damage at the junctions where the legs and tentacles had been removed by the Ooaurs. These cubes could not be equipped again until after necessary repairs had been made to them. While their heads were being placed on new bodies, the two rescued Zoromes related their fight with the Ooaurs and their subsequent adventures.

Meanwhile, the Oaos still hovered on high, and when the spaceship returned to Ui they followed. Twilight had settled beyond the rim. The Oaos did not enter the city, nor did they descend. Darkness finally cloaked them, and neither machine men nor Disci knew if they had departed or not.

Thoughts of the Oaos became suddenly diverted during the night by the appearance of several balls of light falling slowly into the city. The machine men had come to know what this ominous sign meant. The Eiuks were on a raid for tender and delectable Disci. There were five of them, five who had found themselves sufficiently low in generative gas to allow them to settle at this forbidden level. Through some instinctive faculty, they realized the existence of the Uum as their hereditary prey.

The machine men hurried to make short work of the marauders from on high, yet even as 9V-774 stabbed the darkness with a beam from his ray ejector, two of the Eiuks changed from dazzling yellow to a beautiful, emerald glow as jade spots appeared suddenly upon them and merged together. This prismatic metamorphosis rapidly lost its glorifying effect as black spots came into view and grew large where spots of jade had first appeared. Like ebbing rockets, the Eiuks fell into the city, leaving a pungent odor of cinderized flesh. The heat rays of the Zoromes stabbed down two more of the nocturnal horrors from on high, jade spots and heat rays simultaneously attacking the remaining Eiuk. In the waning glow of the final victim, the machine men saw a faint reflection from a metal globe that swooped past. The Oaos had closed for direct hits, leaving no wasted shots as a possible peril to the Uum below.

In the morning, the three Oaos were seen exactly where darkness had come upon them the night before. With the dawn, they suddenly whirled into motion, lowering and circling where the spaceship rested. Then they slowly rose on high, swooping about the ship once more and heading skyward toward the haunts of the Eiuks. It was evident that they wished the machine men to follow.

"In the ship or on the wing?" 20R-654 asked.

"Both," was the professor's reply. "I have an opinion that the Oaos are not going very far, yet they may."

"It is now certain that they cannot communicate telepathically with us," 744U-21 asserted. "Otherwise, they would have done so."

The spaceship rose above the city of Ui, every inhabitant out to watch. Ship and winged escort followed the Oaos, the Zoromes positive that the Oaos were taking them to the latter's homeland, their place of origin. High up into the mountains and still higher the Oaos led them. Soon they were among the lower ranks of the ascending Eiuks. Disregarding the many-tentacled orange globes that were now growing more numerous, the metal balls rose ever higher, penetrating the long field of Eiuks, their highest outpost. The starlit sky became darker as the atmosphere waned. The Oaos entered space, their metal sides more sharply etched where the sun shot dazzling beams of light against their hemispheres.

The flying Zoromes, now aware that the Oaos were capable of space flight, entered their spaceship, and those who left once more to resume their flight with the Oaos donned their temperature equalizers, their vulnerable, organic brains now defying the frigidity of space as well as the burning, concentrated rays of sunlight upon their metal heads.

At length, the Oaos came opposite a yawning cleft between two towering mountain pinnacles of massive breadth, and nearing this they changed their upward ascent to horizontal level so as to pass through.

"They are taking us somewhere beyond the mountains," the professor observed, staring upward at the sunlit crags, the space between the peaks embroidered with stars.

Over the mountain pass glided the mysterious Oaos, followed by a covey of flying Zoromes and their spaceship. They were far above the roof of the world, many miles above the outermost layer of rarified atmosphere. On every side, space enshrouded them in a sunlit night, the bony mountain heights sharply etched where sunlight and shadow clashed unblendingly. The terrain over which they flew was rough, sharp and unweathered, like the surfaces of airless worlds the Zoromes had visited; much like Earth's moon, the professor recollected.

One of the Oaos commenced suddenly to act queerly. It no longer pursued the straight course to which the remaining two globes still held. The metal sphere dipped strangely, side-slipping and rolling in an apparent effort to rise once more to the level of its companions. As the Zoromes flew near, the eccentric globe shot suddenly downward in what the professor divined was not an intentional drop but a direct fall. More than a hundred feet below them lay the base of the enormous cleft, and against the jagged rocks the falling Oao smashed in ruin.

Strangely enough, the Oaos above did not stop to examine their fallen companion but kept on through the pass. As one, the flying machine men darted to the wrecked globe. Its mechanism lay in broken, detached confusion among crushed and ruptured plates of the metal sphere. But nowhere could the machine men discover its inmates. The only remainder suggesting organic habitation was the swiftly-congealed green fluid which lay spattered about in hardened chunks. This the machine men knew as the killing liquid which the Oaos had shot forth among the Ooaurs and Eiuks. Nowere was there the least trace of organic life; all was mechanism, so much of it that the machine men were positive that there existed no surplus room for a passenger of any kind.

"These metal globes are governed by remote control," was 744U-21's ultimatum.

"Come," said the professor. "We must follow."

Already the spaceship was nearly out of sight, still on the track of the remaining Oaos. The flying Zoromes rapidly made up the distance between.

"Why do you suppose the globe crashed?" queried 4F-686.

"Probably because something happened to its mechanism," 12W-62 replied. "The other globes could do nothing for it, and so they kept onward."

Shortly after the machine men had caught up with the spaceship, they saw more of the wrecked globes strewn about the mountain pass. How long they had been there was undeterminable.

"There is probably something about the coldness and lack of air in space which wreaks special havoc with the spheres up here," was the professor's opinion. "It would account for the fact that the two we are now following are progressing at their swiftest pace. They want to be free of here as soon as possible."

"You mean their directors want them free of here," 6W-438 corrected.

"Yes, their directors, whatever manner of things they may be. We have accorded the Oaos separate individualities so long that it is a bit difficult to acclimate ourselves to the idea that they are merely inanimate proxies."

"The directors evidently live on the other side of this lofty mountain range."

Such was the general belief among the machine men of Zor at these latest developments.

Without apparent warning, the cleft merged into a sheer precipice, dropping away for several miles to reveal the country which lay beyond. The Oaos did not descend but still sped straight over the strange country partly veiled

106

by the atmosphere so far below. The machine men could see but little of the topography, for thin clouds hung over the surface.

As if guided by a single thought, the two Oaos dropped quickly toward the ocean of air as they found themselves free of the gaunt mountain peaks. One of them continued to drop so swiftly that the winged Zoromes lost sight of it. The other, though falling at a swift pace, was not difficult to follow. The machine men sensed a subtle anxiety of the globe to be out of space as quickly as it could safely drop. From a telescope aboard the spaceship, 75J-02 announced that the first metal sphere never checked its descent, still hurtling downward at a terrific rate as it pierced the cloud blanket.

"Lost from control," was the professor's thought. "The same fate as those back there in the mountain pass."

Gaining the atmosphere, the single remaining globe checked somewhat its mad descent until it reached the clouds, where it decelerated gradually. For a time the machine men lost sight of the globe, until they, too, had dropped through the clouds. Far to one side lay a city, and further away they could see more of them, tiny and almost phantasmic in the distance.

The globe headed directly for the city, the flying Zoromes and their spaceship flanking the flight of the surviving Oao. Eagerly, the cosmic travelers stared at the spectacle of the city growing rapidly in their vision.

They were scarcely afflicted with surprise through sight of the city, but when cruising slowly above the outlying buildings they gained their first glimpse of the inhabitants, a real mental shock lay in store for them. Organic disks rolled along on many feet, large, staring eyes ogling excitedly at them. The streets and tops of the buildings were full of them. The machine men had evidently been expected; the Zoromes had realized this the moment they had discovered the secret of the Oaos far up in the airless mountain pass. But to find the directors of the mechanical Oaos to be Disci was a feature for which the machine men had never looked.

Conjecture flew thick and fast among the machine men of Zor. What relationship did these Disci bear to the Uum of the city of Ui on the other side of the gigantic mountain range near the world's rim? And why did they send their mechanical spheres over there?

The machine men had lost sight of the lone Oao that had

brought them there. Now they saw more of the Oaos rising slowly to meet them. The attitude of the citizens was all friendship. A large spot was already cleared for the spaceship to land in the center of the city, and at once the machine men realized that these new Disci had perfected television, for the empty spot was one which allowed the spaceship a perfect fit. As the ship settled, the Zoromes became aware of a similarity in the general architecture of the city to the few larger and more elaborate buildings back in the center of Ui. The greatest contrast between the two cities, however, was the lack of a wall here, the machine men noticed.

Crowds of Disci came milling about the ship as it landed, making the air ring with their acclaiming din. It was evident that the machine men were held in high esteem, and probably, the professor thought, because of their befriending the Uum.

"Hail, metal men!"

This was the concensus of the cries arising from the multitudinous Disci. From out of the ship came the Zoromes, while those on the wing settled upon the ship's hull or flew down to the narrow ring of space surrounding the ship, this space commencing to fill with the shoving throngs of Disci.

"What are you to the inhabitants of the solitary city beyond the mountains?" Professor Jameson queried, concentrating his mental faculties to the attunement of the Disci about them.

Many and slightly varied were the excited replies in answer to the startling question which framed itself so unexpectedly in the minds of the Disci.

"Our brethren!"

"The lost nation!"

"Ancestral relatives!"

"The isolated colony!"

And in return, the questions flew thick and fast regarding the machine men.

"Where are you from?"

"What manner of things are you, who are of metal yet are capable of thought projection?"

Out of the confusion, several of the Disci, apparently officials of some importance among their people, stepped out of the crowd and came alongside the gathering machine men.

"We are the Urum," spoke one of the Disci, the machine men divining the perogative to the uttered speech. "You have

108

befriended our unfortunate people beyond the barrier mountains, and therefore we hold you highly in our regard. You have protected our people from the Undum and Elkiri, their natural enemies. Here, we have no fear of the Undum, though the Elkiri occasionally float down to attack us, for species of them live on both sides of the mountains."

At this point, the machine men were aware of vocal appellations dissimilar to those indicative of the Ooaurs and Eiuks of Ui mention.

"How did your people in this lost colony get over the mountains?" asked 744U-21, expecting to hear a tale of lost space navigation. "It must have been a very long time ago, for they have almost forgotten you. You have become but an obscure legend to them. When they die, they believe their souls will float over the mountains.

"Is that so?" queried the Disci. "You see, we have no way of listening to their talk, though with our metal globes we can watch them. Unfortunately, the flight of the globes through space precludes the possibility of transmitting speech, an accomplishment supplementary to television on this side of the mountain. But here—I am failing to answer your questions. How did our inaccessible colony get where it now is? Not over the mountains but under them."

"The old river tunnel!" 6W-438 exclaimed. "We explored it!"

"Yes, so have we—with the metal globes—as far as it goes. I feel that you have now grasped the significance of our relative positions, we and our old colony. Yes, an earthquake destroyed nearly the entire tunnel, even to sealing the entrance at this end. Our colony has not progressed, you have noticed now by comparison with our city. In fact, it has degenerated if anything. Our only contact with them is rather a one-sided affair with the metal globes. They evidently do not understand them."

"You are right." 744U-21 confirmed the latter supposition.

"Tell me," urged the Urum. "How do you think, you things of mechanism?"

"We are not entirely mechanical," replied 744U-21, and he explained their combination of organic brain and metal body.

"Why do you not build the metal spheres large enough to carry yourselves back and forth across the airless voids in the mountains?" the professor suggested.

"We are working upon that," was the answer. "We have worked many long years upon that hope since we first met success in using the metal globes, but so far we have failed. Even our globes are far from what we would like them to be. They become easily unmanageable. You saw what happened to two of them."

"And there were many more high up in the mountain pass in a like condition," the professor added.

"Whenever we can," explained one of the Disci, "we protect our lost colony of Uri from the Elkiri and the Undum. They are no match for our metal spheres."

"So we saw."

"We even attempted to dig out the tunnel, but we gave it up as a hopeless task."

"You felt that more efficient space navigation would be apt to occur sooner?"

"We hope so."

EPILOGUE

The machine men and the Urum learned much from each other. In their brief stay among the Uum, the machine men had discovered many things through conversation that the Urum had not learned in an age of using their mute Oaos. In return, the machine men learned more concerning how Uri, or Ui, had been founded by the ancients, and how several hundreds of them had been destroyed in the tunnel's destruction by a violent temblor. The machine men had found some of the ancient bones in their exploration of the place.

The machine men assisted the Urum in bettering their metal spheres, giving forth all their extensive knowledge of space navigation to aid the perfection of the elementary efforts achieved by the Disci. They learned that the Oaos were kept in the air easily by gaseous principles the Urum had learned from close examination of the Eiuks, but in space another more rapidly exhaustible power was necessary to maintain the Oaos in flight.

The knowledge of the Urum in regard to the world they lived upon was more or less obscure, though they had long ago guessed, through observation of the world's rim bordering the Land of Exhaustion, that their world was strangely unlike the other planets they noticed through their telescopes as circling the same sun. They were also aware, either by traditional word of the ancients, or by instruments contained in the metal spheres, that the gravity beyond the rim was considerably greater than on their own side. The machine men were able to put to rest many of their conjectures and disputes regarding the immense chunk, or cosmic fragment, on which they lived.

Most intriguing of all to the Disci were the trips into space on which the Zoromes conducted them in their spaceship. Several trips were made to Ui, and the Urum from beyond the barrier mountains once more trod the avenues of the walled city after more than a thousand years or more.

With their spaceship, and in company with the Disci, machine men of Zor explored all sides of the planet fragment, and they found strange forms of life, both plant and animal, living in stranger environments. The planet fragment was an interesting freak of the cosmos, and the machine men decided to stay and exhaust its mysteries and natural wonders before moving on again.

On the advice of the Urum and the wishes of the Uum themselves, the latter were all transported by spaceship over the mountains to the motherland, leaving Ui deserted and silent. Ghostly memories flitted there, at night, flaming balls fell from the skies, and the stillness by the base of the mighty peaks was no longer broken by the frightened, agonized shriek of some careless Disc who had not seen fit to close an entrance. The incandescent globes bobbed searchingly in and out of the hollow eyes of the abandoned buildings, heeding the irresistable call of dawn to rise once more, perhaps forever, to the rarified heights of the stratosphere and beyond.

Roving bands of Ooaurs came and hammered madly and unresisted at the massive walls surrounding the city, many of them leaping to the top and dropping within. But they found no prey, only a vast emptiness. Once they had heard cries of alarm and had been met with sharp pikes. Now the tempting, palatable Disci were gone, as if swallowed by eternity. Only silent memories now haunted the deserted city of Ui.

THE MUSIC MONSTERS

I

A PILLAR OF ANGRY FLAME leaped skyward, tinting the
swirling crepe of surrounding smoke and obscuring the figure
which groped its way through the inferno. Above lay darkness, the glitter of the stars softened by the rose-tinged smoke.
The curtain lifted, and again the figure became visible, this
time in the act of leaping over a glowing crevice. Escape
appeared hopeless, for as far as the eye could see—and the
vision was more or less limited—lay the smoldering, glowing
fields of volcanic terrain. Acrid smoke spread the lurid glow
more evenly over the darkened, partly-cooled surfaces from
the heated rivulets and white-hot lakes of fire.

That organic creatures could survive this desolation and
fiery menace for a minute seemed impossible. A missed
step plunged a foot of the wanderer into a glowing hollow
from which it was hastily withdrawn as a drifting pall of
smoke once more enveloped the vicinity. What manner of
creature was this who could venture so carelessly a lower
limb into a red-hot cauldron, withdraw it apparently un-
harmed and stand placidly waiting for the smoke veil to
rise or pass that he might see his way better?

The smoke disappeared slowly, leaving the standing figure
haloed in a hellish glare from which his appearance became
more definite as the filmed veil drifted away. He was a
machine man, a thing of metal. Apparently, unless his parts
heated to the melting point, he had nothing to fear.
This was not so, for despite the temperature equalizer which
fitted so closely down over his metal-coned head, 6W-438
still lay in dangerous prospect of becoming a victim of the
intense heat, the apparatus, though functioning to perfection by supplying the necessary heat in space, did not do
quite so well in reverse as a cooling system, though even
in this latter respect its performances were remarkable.

The machine man of Zor made no move to continue
as the smoke lifted, but stood there firmly upon his four
metal feet, his six tentacles of the same material swinging aim-

lessly from the cube of his metal body. Telepathic thoughts groped through the hell behind him and communed with the unseen. Patiently he stood there as if waiting, and then, dimly at first, more machine men appeared and came to join him. Still more of them came, a few of them helpless and carried by their companions, their feet and legs strangely warped as if subjected suddenly to terrific heat. Others were unconscious, the heat having finally reached and overcome their brains. These latter had their heads detached from their metal bodies, the heads held high in curled tentacles by companions, that they might absorb no more heat and stand a better opportunity of losing that which they had already gathered.

"10B-33 is dead!" 12W-62 exclaimed. "He fell into a lake of fire back aways! We could do nothing to help him, though 7H-88 melted part of a tentacle away reaching for him!"

"777Y-46 nearly went in, too," 41C-98 continued, "but we caught him in time."

"The ground was undermined at the lake's edge," 21MM-392 explained.

The final stragglers appeared, and there were sixteen in all assembled on the cooled knoll where 6W-438 had waited.

"If the spaceship would only land here we might be out of this place safely," said 8L-404. "But 20R-654 does not dare bring it down in here."

"Nor do I blame him."

"Had it not been for the fire-dwellers, we should not have penetrated so deeply into this volcanic country."

"Have you seen them lately?" queried 6W-438.

"No," 119M-5 replied. "We must have shaken them off when we waded through the river of flaming lava. As adapted as they are to the conditions of this place in which they live, even then they dared not duplicate our feat. After all, beneath their thick, asbestos-hided skins, they are organic, and there is a limit to their invulnerability to fire."

"Whoever would have believed that we should have found organic life here in this fire country? We have found strange creatures and strange conditions on this planet fragment, but this has everything else beaten."

"How do these things live?"

"How did the ohbs live?" countered 41C-98, referring to the denizens of another planet in a distant system recently visited by the machine men. "They were organic."

"They ate metal—but you don't believe these things live by absorbing metal?"

"What about fire?"

"Not exactly," said 6W-438. "But the reference to their sustenance on fire approaches a growing theory of mine quite closely. Do you know what I believe they utilize for food?"

"What?"

"From all we have witnessed, not one of us has been able to distinguish a mouth, yet a brief examination of one 21MM392 killed in combat showed an elaborate assortment of ventricles, or nostrils. I believe that they subsist on the sulphurous fumes of the smoke. We have often found them standing motionless and relaxed in dense clouds, and that was one reason we blundered upon them when we might have avoided them."

"We should have brought weapons," advised 119M-5, too late.

"But who expected we would need them here?" asked 92ZQ153. "Instead, we brought the more obvious articles we might use, the temperature equalizers."

"And they have served us well."

"21MM392 has the only weapon among us, his heat ray built into a foretentacle."

"If the spaceship comes low enough, we can order those aboard to drop us weapons."

"We may not need them. The fire-dwellers are behind us. They cannot cross the river of fire as we did—to the detriment of many of our metal legs. Besides, the heat rays seem to have little effect upon them unless we are able to concentrate long enough on one particular spot."

"They may find a way of getting to us again, and how do we know but what there may be some of them on this side of the river we crossed?"

"Now that we have lost 10B-33, 744U-21 may find a way to lower a cable to us from the spaceship by which we might climb up or be hauled up," suggested 21MM392. "He spoke of it when we were last in contact."

"That was before we escaped the fire-dwellers. Two nights and a day have passed since then."

"What savage brutes they are. They picked up red-hot rocks and threw them at us."

"They constitute more of a menace to us than did the Ooaurs, at least under these circumstances," opined 27E-24. "It is more or less synonymous with their great strength

114

that they should live upon the antipode of the Land of Exhaustion. Both sides are of equal gravity."

Standing together, there was nothing by which to distinguish them as the cosmopolitan crew they were. They were sixteen in number; now twenty-two of their companions, the remainder of the expedition under the joint leadership of 744U-21 and 21MM392, were with the spaceship.

The expedition of the Zoromes had experienced several noteworthy adventures on the planet fragment. After exploring one side of the slab, they had turned their attentions to another of the sides and had found a region of fire country, fourteen thousand miles deep. That they had discovered the unexpected and were forced into an unforeseen dilemma is already apparent.

"Are we certain we are traveling in the same general direction?" asked 6W-438. "Otherwise we may never find our way out of this wretched place."

"We have pursued pretty well the same direction, especially at night," said the professor. "I have watched the stars from time to time, keeping one constellation in sight since our escape from the fire-dwellers. When detours around the lakes of fire have taken us on a tangent, we have always swung back again."

"Then we are bound to come out, for though this volcanic country is quite extensive it does not possess unreasonably far boundaries."

"Let us push on again," urged 41C-98. "When dawn comes, we may sight the spaceship again, and they can tell us where we are."

"The last time we contacted them, we were near the center of this fiery morass."

The machine men left the little dark knoll upon which they had stood crowded together, and plunged once more into lurid, apocalyptic nightmare, skirting the yawning, smoking crevices and the pools of molten lava. They often leaped gaping fissures in spite of dangerous, crumbling sides which threatened to precipitate them into the glowing residue at the bottoms. When veils of smoke enshrouded them, they halted, for a false step meant death. Their lower limbs grew intensely hot, creeping heat reaching slowly up to their metal, cubed bodies. It was often necessary for them to wade through shallow pools of glowing lava; there was no other way. When heat threatened to creep up through the metal bodies to the vulnerable brain in its protected cone and temperature equalizer, they were hoisted in strong tenta-

115

cles above the head of a companion, who carried them while they partly cooled off in the absence of contact with the hot ground which they monotonously traveled.

With a lightening on the horizon, the hellish glare of the waste lands became less. The machine men paused in the path of a dense cloud of yellowish, acrid smoke which rolled down upon them in a billowing cloud. They waited for it to roll onward, that they might be sure of where they walked. Near the center of the subdued conflagration, where they had found most of the fire-dwellers, the walking had been less hazardous, for the ground had been less hot and the fire cauldrons there more rare. They had kept on through blinding smoke, but here they dared not risk themselves to chance. The crevices were many and deep, and the reflected glare in the smoke camouflaged any appearances of a glowing trap, for in the smoke it always appeared as if they were in the center of a fiery pit or else near one. They could only be patient and wait upon the vagaries of the source of the smoke or the air currents which directed it.

The smoke pall clung tenaciously, seemingly reluctant to clear away, and during this time the professor realized that with another day soon to break he would lose sight of his guiding star. The rotation of the planet fragment presented a strange solar aspect, and often it was difficult to diagnose directions from the position of the sun. Dawn and twilight were usually drawn-out affairs, for the elongated planet was of such a nature that the sun shone crosswise of the atmosphere on two or more facets all the time. The equator of the rotating fragment girdled it nearly diagonally, so that portions received varying amounts of sunlight. Added to this, the inclination of forty-seven degrees gave it a procession of seasons on its orbit. Being close to the sun, the great fragment revolved rapidly, so that the seasons passed quickly and afforded but little opportunity for the temperature contrast. From an Earthly standpoint, the climate was very hot as the professor knew, but compared to the place they were in now, the general climate of the misshapen planet was that of a veritable polar cap.

The cloud of smoke thinned, and the professor saw his metal companions about him as in a dream haze of subconsciousness. And then he saw something else ahead of them, where the smoke was still dense. There was a scarcely perceptible movement in the depth of the dissipating smoke, but it set in action a vague, uneasy suspicion as the machine men grasped the flash of thought from that one keen observation of Professor Jameson. The smoke thickened. They saw nothing more for several minutes. Then, magically, the smoke cleared away. Before them more than a score of the fire-dwellers threw off their lassitude at sight of them. Mute, they made no sounds. Silent, they set about their grim impulses, with which the machine men were already quite well acquainted.

Other than occasional resort to hurling chunks of rock at the machine men, the fire-dwellers were weaponless. They were nearly as large as the Ooaurs and as strong. The environment of superior gravity was responsible for this. In no way did they resemble the Ooaurs unless their four lower appendages could be likened to those of the antipodes' inhabitants, but, as for the feet, even this slight resemblance became contrary in detail.

The feet of the fire-dwellers were much like those of a horse, the professor had previously observed, the hoof built high into the leg and consisting of a hard, heat-resisting growth. That, too, bespoke adaptation to environment. The four legs supported a bulky, headless body, headless if a neck is necessary to constitute a distinction. Four deeply set eyes in diamond formation occupied the face. This number was necessary to afford sideward vision in the circumstances, for those two in vertical formation were, like the other two, too deeply set to afford other than a straight, limited vision, and all four of the optics were protected in emergency by hard, bony lids. The upper appendages were also four in number, two on each side of the huge, ovoid body, ending in crablike claws of the same substance as the hoof material. These claws were remarkably dextrous at seizing and hurling red-hot chunks of rock.

In color, these veritable Lucifers of the fire country ranged from dark slate to pale green, their hide of a thick, tough substance impervious to any heat other than the brightly glowing lakes of fire from which the machine men had seen them stay clear. The things possessed no mouths, but their entire body, with the exceptions of their eight appendages, were set with some hundred or more perforations through which they evidently breathed, somewhat supporting the theory of 41C-98 and 6W-438 that the fire-dwellers gained sustenance from the acrid smoke of the volcanic terrain.

The machine men already knew the battling tactics of the fire-dwellers; they snapped and tore with their claws and

117

pushed their opponents into the nearest fissure or molten pond handy. They were evidently versed in the art of combat; but the machine men had yet to discover why, unless they battled with each other, for no other creatures occupied this desolate, burning expanse, and it had been argued unlikely that they ever left the fire country. Enabled by nature to stand the intense heat in which they lived, it was by general axiom that lower temperatures must prove fatal to them. On these latter points, the machine men were uncertain.

Fearlessly and in silence, the fire-dwellers charged the metal invaders of their infernal domain, and equally as fearlessly and as silently the machine men resisted the attack of their towering adversaries. For once, the professor's heat ray was more or less of a total loss. No brief sweep or limited concentration on the fire-dwellers had any effect, and the latter were far too active to permit a prolonged focus upon any one part of their anatomy.

Now, in a vicious avalanche, they launched their ponderous bulk upon the lost machine men. Metal tentacles came to grips with rough-skinned arms that possessed an epidermis thicker and more callous than that of the pachyderms which Professor Jameson could recollect on his planet Earth.

"Look for an opening to dash through!" cried 6W-438. "We must try to keep to our original direction!"

"There are no openings! More of the things are coming!"

"They are closing up!"

"Here—this way!" 41C-98 discovered that the horde of the fire country was massing on one side of them and coming forward like a mighty, irresistible wall of brute strength. "Run this way! We may be able to wade another river of fire and elude them!"

In truth, the fire-dwellers had lost any chances they might previously have had of surrounding the machine men, for they were massed to one side. 12W-62, standing nearest them, stood his ground and resisted them momentarily, swinging his lashing tentacles viciously into the approaching fire-dwellers, slashing and cutting obtuse wounds in their tough epidermis, but otherwise wreaking little havoc. One of them seized him and threw him far to one side, where he splashed in a little pool of red-hot lava. Quickly, 12W-62 extricated himself and caught up with his slowly-retreating metal brethren. The fire-dwellers did not seem anxious to catch up with the machine men. That they were the same band that had attacked them before, the machine men were positive, for

118

their actions betokened experience. The fire-dwellers now appeared content to keep the machine men moving in one direction.

Though according the creatures no great intelligence, the professor recognized in this a probably instinctive subtlety. Why were they being herded this way instead of being promptly attacked as before? Of course, the fire-dwellers had not fared so well themselves, for many of their number had been hurled into the lakes of fire where their tough, asbestos skin had availed them no protection whatever.

II

"TURN TO THE LEFT when we reach this rise," the professor told his companions. "Let us see what their intentions are. Run on in the direction they are pushing us, 33F-65, and see if there is any reason why they should herd us that way."

The crowd of menacing fire-dwellers was being constantly joined by more companions. Steadily they forced the machine men to retreat, all the time keeping a closely massed formation; none of them rushed forward alone. Reaching the knoll, the machine men commenced deploying along a ridge at right angles to the direction of their retreat. 33F-65 had disappeared in the smoke. Thick veils rose and hid the oncoming fire-dwellers from time to time, but always it lifted to reveal them once more. A wall of the monsters phalanxed the diverting column of machine men, descending upon 6W-438, who represented the extreme end. The machine man drew back with 9V-774 and 119M-5, and all three at once engaged the pushing, pressing fire-dwellers. There followed a scrimmage in which the fire-dwellers were thrown forcibly off the ridge, but more of the great brutes came, and the machine men were once more forced in their original direction of retreat.

Out of the smoke came crashing a running metal form, vibrating a mental warning. It was 33F-65.

"The ground drops away behind us to a broad pit of flaming lava!"

The professor and many of the Zoromes had expected something like this. They were upon the brink of eternity, for 33F-65 had returned quickly.

"We must retreat no further," 6W-438 warned. "We must charge them and face out the issue."

119

"It is the only thing left to do," said the professor. "Let us form a compact wedge and drive at them."

With orderly haste, the machine men massed themselves and, gathering speed, rammed the very midst of the living wall. Those of the fire-dwellers having the misfortune to be in the way were crushed between the hurtling metal bodies and their companions behind. In the rear of the flying wedge, 41C-98, feeling the force of their momentum checked and spent, hurled himself above his companions and upon the fire-dwellers. Viciously, he flailed with metal tentacles, thoughtfully regretful that these things possessed no necks to choke and strangle. Strong arms reached up and seized him. These in turn he entwined with his tentacles, and a locked struggle ensued. Those creatures behind the main, forward wall pressed forward, felling the struggling antagonists and marching over them irresistibly, driving back the remainder of the machine men in the direction of the flaming pit. Had darkness reigned, this pit might have betrayed its existence by an aura of greater brilliance, but now a murky dawn had succeeded the darkness.

6W-438 felt the impact of many feet. The fire-dweller he held was being trampled to death. But what else was happening, he wondered? Where were his companions? Mentally, he grasped the fact that they were being driven backward toward the fiery cauldron. The fire-dwellers had planned well, yet their insignificant brains seemed devoid of such guile. More likely it was a mechanical instinct, something they had done many times before. The machine men had found it almost impossible to glean information from the minds of these inhabitants of the fire country.

What might have happened to the machine men is problematical, yet it seemed almost inevitable. The machine men, now so close to the edge of the fiery furnace that they were aware of the terrific heat which surged up from below, were about to make another onslaught into the driving wall of fire-dwellers, ready to hurl themselves atop the living ranks, as had 41C-98, in an effort to gain less hopeless positions, when something happened. From above, a blast of power thundered into the close-packed multitude of fire-dwellers. Unnoticed by the desperate combatants below, a small dot had fallen rapidly from above to merge into a growing blot above the milling throng. The spaceship had come and unloosed a blast of destruction as it swooped past, 20R-654 unable to check the terrific momentum. The machine man might have checked the speed almost instantly, but the ship was not in free space; to have done so in the grip of gravity would have proved destructive to the occupants of the ship if not to the ship itself.

Let it be said of the courage, obstinacy or sheer lack of realization on the part of the fire-dwellers, that this preliminary raking fire did not deter them in their fixed design. Many died and more were injured, yet on they surged. The machine men were near to the brink of flaming oblivion, and on came the fire-dwellers. The ship had plunged to the horizon in a terrific, sobbing burst of speed, playing a wailing, fantastic note in the air through which it raced. 20R-654 had the ship veering for a return to the smoking battlefield. Like a mighty, winged phoenix, the spaceship circled widely and returned.

Professor Jameson and his metal companions could feel the terrific heat from beyond the crest to their rear. Smoke partly obscured what lay below, yet the wild, mental flash of 33F-65 had graphically portrayed for them a scene of hellish aspect more than a hundred feet at the bottom of a wide gulf. With 6W-438, 119M-5 and 8L-404, the professor found himself less than ten yards from the brink of this smoking hell. The ground, though hot, was cooler than the air, which would have proved instantly fatal to any organic creatures other than the fire-dwellers, and even they, the professor noticed, were a bit reluctant to pursue their quarry to the edge of the inferno, drawing back instinctively from the withering heat, yet forcing themselves onward through sheer vindictiveness and simple concentration of fixed purpose.

The remaining machine men were mixed among the malignant creatures of the forward wall, fighting with the realization that the spaceship had come to their aid. Not all of the fire-dwellers were willing to brave the terrific heat which smote them so intensely at the edge of the inferno, so that it was no longer a compact wall which advanced upon the four Zoromes, whose companions were now the centers of mixed knots of fighting amid the more compact assemblage of brutes. At a mental instruction from the professor, the four Zoromes stood as if to brace themselves against the expected charge. The fire-dwellers were almost upon the machine men when the latter dodged, and more than half a dozen of the creatures plunged past unblocked, spending their gathered charge in a run and tumble which carried two of them to a flaming death, over the hot, rugged escarpment, into the blazing hell so far beneath. Lurid spray

121

leaped up from the spots where their wildly twisting bodies had ended their long leap. A pall of smoke, swept by chance currents of air, veiled the bubbling, swirling grave of their instant cremations.

As rapidly as they had dodged the charge of the burly fire-dwellers, just so quickly did the machine men follow up their advantage, leaping in upon the tough-skinned creatures and rolling, pushing or hurling them, as the circumstances might warrant, into the pit of fire where the glowing chaos reduced them to smoke and molten ash.

But the fire-dwellers who made up the second and larger group to try to force the machine men off the precipice and into the raging conflagration had seen what ruse the four Zoromes had employed, and they had profited sufficiently to exercise caution. Facing the terrible heat, they came upon the four grouped machine men just as the spaceship returned and wailed past above, spreading another devastating path of death among the evil-tempered denizens of the volcanic country. Still unheedful of the havoc behind them, the fire-dwellers, nearly a dozen strong, threw their bulk upon the four Zoromes and pushed them to the edge of the vast cauldron. Desperately, the machine men gripped their foes. In a death grip, the professor wrestled with two fire-dwellers who were jointly attempting to perpetrate their hideous design. Step by step, they were forcing him backward. With sinking hope, he saw 8L-404 shaken loose from his hold and pushed over the brink of the chasm, the far side of which none of them had yet been able to perceive through the wandering vagaries of the smoke. 119M-5 rolled on the ground securely at grips with one of the fire-dwellers, while two more tried to pull the machine man away. 6W-438 had taken a hold on the first lumbering brute to close with him, turning deftly and pushing him over into the fate the other had meant for him.

All this the professor saw as the two fire-dwellers half pushed, half lifted him to the edge of the flaming holocaust. He swung out over the smoke-veiled sea of fire, yet his hold was so secure as not to be shaken loose. The spaceship was circling above. 20R-654 had slackened the tremendous speed, and the artilleryman now picked off groups of the fire-dwellers where there would be least danger to the scattered machine men.

With a desperate twist of his mechanical strength, Professor Jameson hurled one of his opponents to the ground, falling upon him, dragging the other with him. All three clung together tightly. One of the fire-dwellers, the one on the side away from the inferno below, saw the opportunity of rolling the machine man over the edge, disregarding the fact that his companion was well entangled in the metal tentacles. It may have been forgetfulness, or sacrifice occasioned by the alarming circumstances and the excitement, or it may have been because of the intense heat. No one ever knew. The crazed fire-dweller shoved both machine man and companion over the brink and into the smoke-filled hell beneath, but, as they rolled over, a desperate, grappling arm of the doomed fire-dweller chanced upon the leg of his companion, who was dragged after them, clawing and seizing frantically for pockets and projections where there was naught but slightly roughened rock. All three disappeared from sight.

Meanwhile, the spaceship was taking wholesale toll of the fire-dwellers, forcing upon their sluggish sensibilities the realization that here lay only extermination and defeat. They finally recognized disaster in the circling hull overhead, and they strove to escape it. Fleeing in scattered directions, they sought the densest clouds of smoke, and those who remained in the open found burnt-out crevices in which to hide or else stopped suddenly quiet, their gray bodies merging harmoniously with the barren, desolate landscape and the scattered wisps of smoke.

The machine men collected together beneath the protection of the spaceship overhead and quickly discovered the absence of Professor Jameson and 8L-404. In a body, they walked to the edge of the fiery pit where 6W-428 and 119M-5 had narrowly escaped being thrown to their doom over the precipice with 21MM392 and 8L-404.

"Here was where they disappeared," said 119M-5, once Zora of the Zoromes. "21MM392 took two of the fire-dwellers with him."

While they gazed over the brink, the smoke lifted, and scarcely thirty feet below they saw an inert fire-dweller stretched out upon a narrow, jutting ledge. Another of the dead brutes hung motionless, half over the edge. And then they saw a coned metal head, and a cry of glad recognition swelled up in their minds.

"I am safe. Have the fire-dwellers gone?"

It was 21MM392. He had apparently struck the ledge. Again the smoke obscured him, but not before the machine men from above had noticed the crushed condition of the fire-dweller who lay in from the edge of the ledge. Before

123

the machine men could make comment, the professor issued another startling and unexpected statement.

"8L-404 is down here with me but is unconscious. He must have struck his head a bit. It is not damaged outwardly, however. One of the fire-dwellers broke my fall for me."

When the smoke lifted again, the professor stood alone upon the ledge. Evidently, he had thrown his late opponents to the molten jaws of the glowing fire pot. 8L-404 was propped out of sight against the receding wall of the precipice.

From above in the spaceship, 744U-21 gained contact with those below, learning of what had happened. A length of cable was dropped so that the machine men were able to hoist the professor and the still unconscious 8L-404 out of the scorching hole into which they had nearly been thrown to their deaths.

"There is no near place in this fire country where we dare to land," said 744U-21, "but luckily you are not far from clear ground. You have nearly crossed the fire country. Follow the flight of the spaceship, and we will guide you out."

Though the trip had been a long and arduous one, the following of the stars at night had brought them in a straight line to a position not far from the edge of the volcanic region. They were soon to be rid of the eternal fires. Picking up their crippled companions—who had also taken part in the recent conflict through necessity of self-defense—and carrying the unconscious 8L-404, the machine men trudged on over this heated terrain of smoking crevices and molten rivulets.

"I recollect seeing the land to the other side of the fire country from far above," said the professor. "What is it like? Is it inhabited?"

"It is inhabited," replied 744U-21 from the spaceship. "That we already know. But we know nothing concerning the inhabitants. The land is much like that we explored before you entered the volcanic badlands. It is well wooded and given up almost entirely to dense vegetation. We could see no cities, so the inhabitants must be of a savage or a barbaric nature."

"I hope they are peaceful, or else not as hard to handle as are the fire-dwellers," 6W-438 remarked. "I am tired of physical combat for the time being."

As the machine men progressed, they noticed that the molten lakes and crevices of fire became less numerous, and the smoke clouds became less. Finally they were able to glimpse occasional views of the country bordering the wastelands of fire, and they were gladdened to know that soon they would be free of the treacherous fire country where they had lost one of their number and had nearly been done for, one and all. It was still a long way to walk over arid desolation after they had left the last bit of smoking ground, but eventually an area of bush-growth and a forest in the background greeted them. Here the spaceship had landed. 8L-404 recovered shortly before they reached the spaceship. The last he had recollected was plunging over the edge of the precipice bordering the lake of fire. The smoky haze had enveloped him, and he had felt his tentacles clash against something just a split second before oblivion had enveloped him.

At the spaceship, the crippled machine men were repaired, exchanging warped and misshapen legs, blued and partly melted by the heat, for new ones. A few tentacles needed replacement, but it was mostly the legs that were damaged from walking too often through the lava beds and molten pools.

With ten companions, the professor started for the forest. The party of eleven was progressing through the semi-arid bush land, less than a quarter of a mile from the forest, when several indistinct flickers of motion appraised them that they had been seen and were being carefully watched. Bushes far ahead of them quivered perceptibly from time to time, and the vigilant eyesight of the Zoromes saw slinking forms darting in and out of the forest from time to time. More of them seemed to leave the forest than entered it, the professor observed.

"What are they?"

"We could see but little of them from above in the spaceship," said 744U-21. "We caught no more glimpses of them than we do now."

"They are hiding, but not running from us."

"It looks as if they were trying to ambush us," 29G-75 observed. "It is well that we brought along the ray ejectors from the spaceship."

"They are sneaking from bush to bush; they are coming nearer."

In truth, this was so. Yet the creatures skulked so close to the ground and moved so swiftly that the machine men could gain only an obscure idea of their shape and proportions. They were more than half the distance from the spaceship to the forest when faint sounds broke in upon their hearing. Flutelike notes they were, possessing a variance in scale. They apparently came from the forest. Following a moment's extended silence, an aria of the musical notes burst forth again as in wild melody.

As the machine men continued their walk in the direction of the forest, this simple melody was repeated again and again as if joined by many instruments of the same kind. It seemed a musical chant of sad warning. That was what the professor gathered from it, and he found that his metal bretheren were similarly affected by the haunting music. Still they continued. The weird harmony now assumed a new note, one of mingled defiance and warning. Plainly, the machine men were being warned to proceed no further. As they did not cease their stride, the music grew threatening and wildly exhilarating, and the harmony was broken by variant fancies of tone, merging into a martial phantasm of melody. In it there existed a questioning lilt, and, as if in reply, there broke forth from the scattered bushes, just ahead and to each side of the machine men, an astonishing volume of operatic reply.

"They must carry musical instruments of a sort," 744U-21 commented in surprise. "That is indeed strange."

"And they are a menace," added the professor, "if we are to interpret their renditions correctly."

III

THE AIR RANG with a combined symphony which reminded the professor of latter bars in the *Poet and Peasant Overture*. At a certain point in the warlike song, out from the concealing bushes sprang a representative horde of the things 744U-21 had said inhabited the vast forests stretching away from the fire country into the limitless back country beyond. Possessing long, angular bodies and long, pointed faces, they were supplied with many short legs running up the sides of their bodies. There were fully a dozen of these, the professor's first glance estimated. They walked erect on the lowest pair of these legs, which were three times as long as the other legs. The machine men now understood how these creatures could move so rapidly along the ground and keep out of their sight. The professor visioned them as something like thousand-legged caterpillars standing erect on two legs longer than the others, their bodies surmounted by heads appearing much like a fox's except for the absence of the long, pointed ears. On second sight, the upper legs were not entirely legs, even as the feet of a monkey are not entirely feet. They could be used for holding something, as was evident, for many of these monsters carried long, curved hooks of what appeared to be crudely hammered metal.

Menacingly, they ran to meet the machine men, making the air ring with their fierce music. And now the machine men of Zor were in for another surprise. The melodious sounds did not issue from instruments but from the throats of the monsters themselves.

Approaching nearer, the creatures paused suddenly, and their song changed, became garbled in disorderly chaos as if many of them had suddenly disagreed as to the proper selection. Reading their minds, which the machine men gratefully found to be not only of an open, orderly nature but also receptive to their mental attunement, they found that the strange things were stricken with awe and surprise. They had evidently just discovered that the machine men of Zor were not what they had expected them to be. In their minds, the machine men saw that they had been mistaken for a roving band of the fire-dwellers. The monsters from the forest hesitated uncertainly, giving the machine men an opportunity for conciliatory measures.

"We, too, are enemies of the fire-dwellers," the professor impressed upon them. "We were attacked by them and fought them in the midst of the fire country."

Musical bits interposed upon the silence fallen among the many-legged creatures, and it was apparent that they were conversing, that they always talked to music. Penetrating their thought-train, the machine men found them to possess a crude, barbarous intelligence, far above that of the fire-dwellers. Surprise and greater awe were set to melody in the exchanges between the music monsters, and in it there was mingled respect, respect tinged, however, with suspicion and distrust. This the machine men promptly allayed.

"We wish to be friendly with you," 29G-75 offered.

"Where are you from, and what are you?"

This was the general, unuttered consensus of the attitude directed at the machine men, which, though unvoiced, lay naturally uppermost in the minds of the creatures.

"We are things made of metal, like those weapons you carry for attack on the fire-dwellers," said 744U-21, having already divined the purpose of the hooks. "We come from a world far beyond this one."

Although this information was mostly lost upon the restricted understanding of the music monsters, the simple, straightforward reply to their questions caused a better feeling and relaxation of suspicion. They approached, slowly and wondering, all eyes intent in observing these new, strange things, the machine men.

The machine men engaged them in thought exchange, impressing upon them that, although their musical utterances were peculiarly expressive of their thoughts and attitude, the machine men found their thoughts much more legible.

"What is that huge bird that flew down out of the sky?" one of the music monsters asked.

"It is our spaceship in which we travel. Like our bodies, it is mechanical.

Part of this was understood. The creatures seemed satisfied.

"You fought our enemies, the fire-dwellers?" came the next query. "Did they try to push you into the fires or break your bones with their powerful, crushing arms?"

"They tried to push us into their lakes of fire," Professor Jameson replied. "We are too strong for them to crush, and even should they accomplish this and reduce our bodies to junk, our heads would live on as long as they remained undamaged."

"They are our natural enemies," were the thoughts of the music monsters reduced to words. "We fight each other continually. Sometimes they conduct raiding parties up out of their natural element, coming into the forest after us. Then again, we sometimes penetrate the fire country for a distance and war upon them. Neither of us can enter the other's domain for long. We cannot stand the heat; they cannot exist very long without it."

"Nor without the sulphurous fumes they breathe," added 41C-98 in an aside to his companions.

"Of the two factions, they have the advantage of greater security, for they can go into parts of the fire country where we cannot go even though we are garbed in the heavy pelts of slain fire-dwellers. They can come anywhere in our country until the prolonged lack of heat drives them back again. We, however, overwhelm this advantage of theirs in this respect: that we are a superior race and know how to do things they cannot think to do."

The music monsters proudly exhibited their weapons.

"We also live in communities; the fire-dwellers do not. They wander aimlessly without homes. We move from place to place occasionally, it is true, but we always build. We do not live in the open as they do!"

While the music monsters were eager to demonstrate their superiority over the fire-dwellers, it struck 6W-438 as strange that since it had been the belief among them that the fire-dwellers lived on the fumes of the fire country and did not derive gastronomic sustenance form organic sources, why should they battle the music monsters other than in self-defense? 6W-438 asked as much, although in his mind the suspicion of the truth lurked in his recollection of the attack on the machine men by the fire-dwellers, but he was not yet positive.

"Why do the fire-dwellers come out of their country to fight you?"

"To kill us."

"But why should they? What is there for them to gain?"

"It has always been so."

One of the more astute among the creatures afforded a more satisfactory answer.

"They are of a perverse, cross-grained nature. They would not leave us in peace, even were we to do so by them. It is their nature."

"And why do you enter their country to fight them?" 744U-21 asked. "What, besides vengeance, prompts you to endure the discomforts and hazards of the fire country?"

"We value their pelts. We have many uses for them, principally as a method of barter. Then, we too like to fight, and the fire-dwellers furnish a worthy excuse."

The machine men, though admiring the various qualities of the music monsters, felt that less worthy excuses might suffice them were it not because of defense that they fought the fire-dwellers. It struck the professor that the main reason why the fire-dwellers could not stay out of their fire country for too long a time was not because of the eventual penetration of cold through their thick pelts, though this may have been a secondary reason, but the fact that the fire-dwellers grew hungry for the dense clouds of sulphurous smoke in their natural environment.

Sending back a messenger to acquaint those at the spaceship with the fact that the inhabitants of this new territory were friendly to them, the machine men proceeded onward into the forest with the music monsters. They found the forest aisles neatly kept, and here they learned that the music monsters were strict vegetarians, living on the smaller growth, eating certain kinds of soft wood and various kinds of bark. Their domiciles were found to be small constructions of baked mud held together with twigs, an occasional branch being used, especially in the arched ceilings. They were much more orderly and better made than those of the Ooaurs.

The machine men were struck with the novelty of musical discourse among the barbaric creatures. Always were their musical utterances, even the most commonplace, harmonious. It surprised the professor how many types of Earth's instruments the sounds resembled. The commonest resemblance was to the notes of a flute; then there were many whose utterances sounded as if drawn from quick manipulations of a violin bow. Deeper voiced specimens among the music monsters imitated unwittingly the tones of an oboe or bass viol. Rarer specimens of sound duplicated the harp, guitar, trombone and piccolo. Clarinet voices were common, though nowhere could the professor find any voice resembling a piano, organ or cornet. Strange to say, the music monsters placed no value on their various abilities nor did they seek to cultivate or exercise them in any manner. Familiarity had bred contempt.

Instead, a ludicrous paradox existed in the fact that the only sounds the music monsters made for musical enjoyment were dull, rhythmic sounds on hollow trees accompanied by a maddening, monotonous drone, all in one key.

Strange memories often leaped into the professor's mind across the gap of forty million years, as various couplets of musical conversation accidentally struck a passage of music familiar to him in the long, long ago. Once there had come a fleeting bar of "Lohengrin," then again an incongruous portion of "Turkey in the Straw." Often he was reminded of some old air the title of which he had long forgotten. In discoursing on how the pelts of the fire-dwellers were cured after a raid and cut up into medium of exchange, a music monster had hit accidentally upon a bar of "God Save the King." 119M-5, not so far removed from the prime of an organic existence, recognized passages of music similar to those which had been heard or sung on the planet Zor. The passages, of course, were incomprehensible and unconnected with the rest, as far as the professor was concerned, even as to 119M-5 were the similarities detected by the professor.

The machine men had decided to stay among their

new acquaintances for a short time. The spaceship had been moved up to the edge of the forest, where several of the machine men were always stationed with it, having a good number of the curious music monsters for company. The latter stood in awe of this great flying thing, into which they were allowed to enter. Several of them possessed the life-long boast of having ridden in it as it was moved up from the edge of the fire country to the forest.

One intelligent music monster the professor had dubbed Arminia in his own mind and recognized him as such through the fact that when his companions spoke, or rather sang, his name, the notes duplicated perfectly the opening bars of a song the professor had known by that title.

The music monsters possessed one characteristic which struck the professor as singular: they were inveterate gamblers, employing a number of ways to play games. Not only did they gamble the valuable squares of thick hide they used as common barter, but also gambled freely with their weapons, mates, offspring and even their own services, gambling themselves into virtual slavery for certain periods of time. Often this gambling was diverted from chance to skill in the uncanny casting of their hooks into trees at a considerable distance, but generally they employed a numeric hazard, or guessing. Their chief means of chancing consisted of dice or else the old method of heads or tails, using one or several pieces of metal with distinguishing characteristics, symbols, or crude attempts at illustrative art on either side. Strangely enough, they never employed these pieces of metal as a medium of exchance. The dice were very large and crudely wrought of metal, the music monsters usually employing but one at a time.

On the dice were various symbols, including a poorly sketched fire-dweller, the sun, the jagged-edged moon of the planet fragment, a tree, a prominent constellation of stars peculiar to this perspective of the universe, and the sketch of a music monster. Characteristic of the ego in the music monsters, the representative of their own race on the metal dice signified the fullest value, while the other five illustrations and symbols decreased in value down to the fire-dweller, whose likeness was roundly cursed in musical blasphemy by whoever's misfortune it was to turn up that particular side. Obviously, these crudely constructed dice were imperfectly balanced and played heavy favorites. Closely associated with this uncertainty and fervor of gambling were the accompanying brawls, for many of the music monsters

131

were not loath to cheat. Such differences, however, rarely led to fatality, for the creatures were constrained by accepted law not to use their hooks on each other; they employed instead a rough and tumble mode of fighting, and featured a grappling and pummeling of each other with their many feet.

The villages of the music monsters were open parks amid the dense forests; the various communities were located within a few miles of each other. Comparatively, the extensive forests were quite populated, and clear, wide avenues of parkland stretched like highways, linking up the villages as ways of travel back and forth. The machine men spent most of their time close to the frontier bordering the wastelands. Those in the interior rarely saw the fire-dwellers unless they visited a border village close to the fire country. Therefore, the border villages contained the more adventuresome types to be found among the music monsters.

One night, Professor Jameson and three companions and several of the music monsters were gathered close by the spaceship in the dim light of the rugged moon. From the fire country came a lurid yet less illuminative glare. In the spaceship were three more of the machine men. All seven consisted of the inevitable watch left with the ship. The rest of the Zoromes were scattered about the neighborhood of the forest, most of them in the nearest village.

The music monsters were gambling. Looking on, and furnishing an aura of illumination with their body lights, were the professor, 4F-686, 41C-98 and 12W-62. Arminia and four companions were the gamesters, and the large dice had not done so well by Arminia. He had lost his squares of hide, and now he was risking something he did not yet possess, but which had been promised him. The music monster had been desirous of a ride in the spaceship clear across the fire country. This had been the height of his ambitions, and the machine men had promised that he would be one of the villagers to be taken aloft the next time the spaceship rose. Secretly, the machine men had something better in store for the music monsters than a mere ride over the fire country and back. They would keep on going all the way around the planet fragment, coming back by circumnavigation.

Now, Arminia was gambling his chances of the coveted ride with a companion who had willingly massed a recently acquired pile of hide barter, some of it having previously been in the possession of Arminia, as a stake. The dice rolled. Up came the tree. This was arbitrary in the fact that it called for a further side bet, holding the original stake in suspension. Arminia had nothing left to bet. The cast was disregarded, and now it was Arminia's turn to roll the cube. He hesitated, juggling the dice preliminary to throwing, and then with fatalistic resignation twirled and let roll. The dice stopped, and the poorly executed likeness of the fire-dweller stared mockingly at Arminia. He had lost, and the stake set up by the other gamesters was being returned to a huge pouch carried by the music monster. Just then a commotion in the direction of the spaceship attracted the attention of them all, players and spectators.

Simultaneously, there flashed into the minds of the machine men an electrifying communication from the spaceship. Already they were cognizant of the circumstances of which the music monsters were soon to know.

"Fire-dwellers! In the spaceship!"

"A raid of the fire-dwellers!" the professor attuned his thoughts to the perceptibilities of the five music monsters. "Come quick!"

Machine men and their allies raced to the dark-looming hull between them and the volcanic region. Limned against the lurid background of the fire country were the dark bodies of the fire-dwellers, surging in large numbers toward the spaceship. The machine men headed for the entrance and found a closely-packed mass of the fire-dwellers before them. Inside, the professor knew, were 29G-75, 948D-21 and 454ZQ2. Shining their body lights upon the milling throng and beyond to the side of the ship, the machine men were appalled by the large number of attacking brutes. In the dim light of the moon, and against the red glare of the fire country, they saw many bobbing forms and knew that more of the dread creatures were racing across the barren plain.

"Get to the doorway and enter the ship!" the professor told his companions and allies. "We must hold it in defense until reinforcements come from the village!"

Many of the fire-dwellers were stamping on in the direction of the forest, but most of them were gathering around the ship. Already, the machine men and music monsters were hemmed in by the increasing numbers of the raiding masses from out of the infernal region. Silent and grim they were, intent only on death and destruction. The music monsters fought madly, ripping and tearing with their hooks, fighting even nearer the ship in company with the machine men. Fire-dwellers were pouring into the spaceship when the professor fought his way to the open doorway. Immediately behind him, Arminia raised a gleaming hook and sank it expertly into the diminutive brain of a fire-dweller who sought to block the machine man. All four of the Zoromes were flailing with their tentacles.

IV

THE PROFESSOR urged Arminia into the ship ahead of him and turned to find that only two other music monsters were still alive in the press of fighting. The last two had succumbed beneath overwhelming waves of their enemies. Had the fighting been more open and in less restricted quarters, doubtless the surviving three would have been killed, but in the pressing multitude only a few of the brutes from the volcanic country could reach them at once, and these were hampered by lack of room. With their wicked hooks, the two music monsters were viciously slashing to right and left.

Holding the doorway with his intense heat ray, Professor Jameson covered the rear of the two music monsters, who made their way to the entrance and leaped inside. Far back, three machine men were battling closer to the ship. The professor now directed his heat ray upon those who blocked their way.

With a lunge, the nearest one, 4F-686, stumbled and caught the edge of the doorway—and then many things happened. Rough, asbestos-skinned arms closed around the professor's body from inside the spaceship, just as the ship gave a jolt and leaped upward violently. 4F-686 was lifted high above the ground as his grappling tentacles slid over the edges of the doorway and he fell downward upon the heads of the milling fire-dwellers whose pressing ranks closed involuntarily upon the opening left by the ship. As the spaceship rose crazily, and the professor tried to throw off the encumbering bodies which held him to the flroor, from out of the forest raced a mixed throng of music monsters and machine men in answer to the call of those aboard the ship. Only momentarily did they pause to consider the receding spaceship, and then they threw themselves into the belligerent fire-dwellers, whose profuse numbers now threatened the villages.

From the open doorway of the ship, Professor Jameson's

apex eye caught a reeling panorama of fire country. Rough, groping paws with long, horny claws felt for a hold, lifting him up. Wildly, he struck out with his tentacles, as he realized they were trying to throw him out through the doorway to the ground a thousand feet below. The ship was now rising faster. His heat ray found a rough body and a bit of concentration penetrated the thick hide, causing muffled snorts of pain from the tiny apertures all over the creature's body. Broken away from the insidious grip, the professor quickly closed the door, knowing full well that the limited intelligence of the great, dumb brutes would not be able to fathom its operation. Again the heat ray played out, bringing whistling noises from the many victims. The fire-dwellers withdrew, the professor moving slowly along behind them. They made a quick charge at him, and, realizing that he must form some plan of action at once, the professor leaped nimbly past them and clanged shut another door, sealing them in the compartment.

The fight which ensued was a monotonous yet grim combat. Knowing that the ship was overrun with the fire-dwellers against four machine men and three music monsters, the professor had closed off all further interruption by shutting the door leading into the depths of the ship. Knowing that the huge, strong creatures could do him no lasting harm, and intent upon slowly beating them down, the professor charged in and grappled with one, while the remaining two, as he had anticipated, flung themselves upon him. It became a tiresome contest of trying to get his heat ray directed against a vital portion of one of the things and killing the creature, thus cutting down the opposition of two. Had they been ordinary organisms, the heat ray would have accomplished swift work, but these Lucifers had lived close to fire all their lives. Pulled off and flung down, the professor was making little headway. Occasionally, when the opportunity offered, he picked up one of them and hurled the brute against the wall head foremost. This induced a dazed condition, but it also gave the fire-dwellers the same idea, and the professor had to cling to them desperately to frustrate their design. How he wished he had one of the music monsters' hooks that were so peculiarly adapted to killing fire-dwellers. He had already flailed their outer hide to ribbons, and it looked as if that were the only effective way, other than getting in intensive work with the heat ray, which was difficult, opposed as he was to the three of them. During grappling deadlocks with the three beasts, he had exchanged mental communication with the other Zoromes, acquainting them with his own dilemma and learning of theirs.

"The spaceship is alive with the fire-dwellers!" 29G-75 exclaimed. "There are at least twenty of them aboard!"

"The ship is still rising!"

"We have shut ourselves off in a separate compartment even as you did, 21MM392. We believe that soon the fire-dwellers must die through lack of sustenance."

"But what of the music monsters?" the professor queried, trying earnestly to bring his heat ray to bear consistently upon the head of a fire-dweller who sat upon his metal cube while another kicked at his head. "They will die, too."

"No—they claim that they can go several days without food, while the fire-dwellers die after more than a day and a half away from their fire country."

"What made the ship rise?"

"The fire-dwellers tampered with and broke some of the controls. The ship is rising and drifting. We are a long way from the fire country by now."

"We are in space," added 948D-21. "We just left the boundaries of the outer atmosphere."

Instantly, the professor conceived an answer to the problem before him. Winning free of the brutes who were trying to bend his legs, he rushed to the side of the ship nearest the door. He could walk, and he had all of his tentacles. The professor was thankful that these inhabitants of the smoking wastelands were not quite as powerful as the Ooaurs had proved themselves to be. He turned a lever just as the determined creatures made another charge for him. They seemed tireless. A faint hissing, to which they paid no heed, became audible. The fire-dwellers soon began acting strangely. They seemed to weaken and weave deliriously. The professor slipped clear of them, watching them intently and waiting. He slid along the wall, his metal body rasping faintly as one of the stupid beasts charged on wavering feet. Raising a metal foot, the professor shoved him to the floor.

The faint hissing continued. The air was leaving the compartment, slowly dissipating itself into space above the planet fragment. All three of the fire-dwellers were breathing in labored gasps, their many ventricles swelling and dilating to suck in the precious, rarefied gas which was becoming still rarer. They could hardly move.

Certain that no longer would the evil, stubborn creatures be capable of a concerted rush upon him, the professor opened the door and stood looking out into the abyss of the stars and reflected sunlight off the planet fragment. A magnificent panorama lay far below, one-half of the broad fragment slowly turning toward the drifting ship, the sunlight creeping up the right-angled side ready to flash simultaneous daylight all over the facet it was gradually approaching. Still above, yet to one side, surrounded by the fiery stars, there shone the jagged moon. The air left much faster through the open door, and the intense cold of space pushed in to replace it.

The professor lost no more time. Seizing the leg of an inert, stiffening fire-dweller, he dragged the body to the doorway and sent it gyrating off into the gravitational grip of the planet fragment. Another body followed the first on its long plunge into territory it had never known in life. The third body the professor heaved toward the doorway where it struck the threshold and glanced out into nothingness. Immediately, he slammed shut the door, for he had no temperature equalizer. The machine men had removed these on leaving the fire country. They were stored in other parts of the ship.

The thought struck him that were it not for the music monsters aboard, the machine men could eject all air and heat from the ship and put on the temperature equalizers, instantly killing the many fire-dwellers still on board. There came an afterthought, that, if the circumstances should become too alarming, the music monsters might have to take their chances with the adoption of such a plan, keeping to a single, air-filled compartment.

"I have disposed of three fire-dwellers," the professor informed his companions in the distantly removed compartment where they held siege. "How many more are there?"

"At least fifteen," 948D-21 replied. "We can hear them moving about the ship. Their attitude seems to be changing. They are becoming confused and scared."

"Are they in the control room?"

"Yes, but we are only waiting until the greater number of them go to other sections of the ship. Arminia says that he and his companions can overcome several of them with our help. We are waiting for the most propitious moment. If we can isolate half of them, we are confident of overcoming the remainder even though they outnumber us."

Patiently, the machine men and their peculiarly valuable allies, the music monsters, waited for their chance. Intense mental concentration of the machine men into the weak, muddled minds of the fire-dwellers kept them constantly appraised of the number of the latter in the control room. Curiosity occasionally led the fire-dwellers to other sections of the derelict craft, yet always there remained an overwhelming number in the control room. After the first clash with the machine men, there had been no more damage to the governing mechanism. The brutes were far too bewildered to consider vandalism and too awed to tamper with the already broken controls which they did not understand.

The music monsters were having a good time. The fluctuating numbers of their enemies in the control room, and the decision to attack with the best odds available, appealed to their gaming nature. Arminia was especially exultant. Fate had oddly twisted the apparent course of events. He had lost on a gamble his chance to ride in the spaceship, yet here he was; but like an evil omen, the fire-dweller's caricature, turned up on the dice, had immediately cast him into alarming circumstances with many of these enemies.

The professor waited for the moment when he should hear them ready for the rush on the control room. There was nothing he could do. Only seven fire-dwellers remained in the control room. Three machine men and three music monsters suddenly rushed the dazed and unsuspecting denizens of the volcanic country. Through the minds of his mechanical brethren, Professor Jameson gained a picture of the fray. 454ZQ2 shoved one of the brutes out a doorway and closed the entrance, while his companions closed the remaining entrances. The music monsters swung lustily with wicked hooks. It was soon over.

Invulnerable to attack, after closing off all chances of help from the rest of the fire-dwellers, the machine men engaged them, while from prearranged plans the three music monsters went around swiftly and cut down the antagonists of the machine men with their sharp hooks. One of the music monsters was seized and crushed by two of the fire-dwellers. His death was avenged six-fold as the rest of the cornered brutes were cut down. Seizing the hook of the dead music monster, 454ZQ2 quickly realized its uselessness in his own unpracticed grasp. For one thing, it required the peculiar grip of the music monster, and it also required knowledge and skill of where and how to hit. After a few ineffectual rips into the tough hide of a fire-dweller, the machine man threw it down in disgust.

Six bulky corpses lay on the floor of the control room.

Eagerly the professor waited for the examination of the controls.

"They are in bad shape, 21MM392," was the ultimatum of 29G-75. "There will be the necessity of many repairs to them."

"Can the ship be guided?"

A moment's pause followed as the machine men in the control room made a few trials. The answer came ominous and disappointing.

"We have no control over the ship at all. It has ceased to rise. We are being held by the gravity of the planet fragment and shall probably rise no higher."

"What are we to do regarding the rest of the fire-dwellers?" queried 948D-21.

"Now that we have the control room in our possession, we can afford to wait and let them die," the professor stated.

"What of Arminia and his companion? There is no food for them here, and besides, after a time, if we are to continue to drift in this manner, the air will have become too noxious for them to breathe."

"Food will be the problem," said the professor. "They will be dead of starvation long before the air in these many chambers becomes unbreathable."

"They may have to digress from their vegetable diet when they become sufficiently hungry," suggested 454ZQ2, his thoughts touching lightly on the six dead fire-dwellers.

The professor also thought of the remaining survivors of the attacking band that had entered the spaceship.

"We still have meat on the hoof, too, you know," he offered jokingly, yet as always his humor escaped the understanding and appreciation of his companions.

It elicited but a sober reflection from 454ZQ2.

"When I was a triped on the planet of the double sun, I ate the meat of lesser creatures and enjoyed it."

"On my world," reminisced the professor, "there were savage tribes who ate the meat of their betters and also enjoyed it."

"The spaceship may come down," said 948D-21.

The machine men debated their situation, occasionally attuning their thoughts to those of the music monsters on some subject of common bond and mutual understanding. Meanwhile, they waited for the fire-dwellers to die. At times they heard them roaming about the spaceship. Never did they try to force the entrances of the control room. The dim-witted creatures of the outdoors did not understand doors any more than they did the walls. To them, an entrance was a hole. Even had they known the use of the doors, however, their combined bulk could not have forced them open.

The possibilities of their having to subsist on sustenance furnished them by the bodies of the fire-dwellers disgusted the music monsters, yet when their grave future was thoroughly explained to them they became partly reconciled to the prospects of such a diet. Both, however, claimed they must become very ravenous before they would yield to this alternative to starvation. They hated the fire-dwellers as a menu as they hated them as neighbors. There was only one use, perhaps two, which the music monsters had for them: their hides and as a quarry in hunting and war.

Finally, the steps of the fire-dwellers were silenced. Not until then did the machine men and their two allies go in search of them. Professor Jameson, in hastening to join his companions in the control room, stumbled over one of the fire-dwellers in the passage outside the compartment where he had been waiting. A cursory examination proved the creature to be entirely inanimate. The luckless fire-dwellers were found all over the ship in strange positions, dead. One stood on its feet, sprawled against the wall. Several of them sat on the floor of the supply room—facing each other with spare mechanical legs of the machine men between them, as if even in death they pondered this puzzling, unanswerable enigma. Only one of fourteen fire-dwellers did the machine men find alive, and he was breathing his last when they discovered him.

The machine men, on the advice of the professor, took the dead fire-dwellers to the nearly airless chamber where he had recently bested three of their enemies, and the remainder of the atmosphere still lingering in the chamber was released. Back in the control room once more, the two music monsters optimistically commenced gambling over the pelts of the twenty fire-dwellers, feeling themselves potentially wealthy. Little did they seem perturbed over the uncertain future they faced, no more anxious than the machine men who were constantly facing such circumstances. Yet the machine men had more concrete basis for their fearlessness. They were not flesh and blood.

The spaceship drifted on toward one end of the planet fragment, continuing at the same level. The professor estimated that they were fully eighty miles above the planet's surface, far above the last remnant of outer air. Already, they had floated close enough to the end of the fragment to look down into the cross-section of atmosphere of the end territory.

"What do you expect will happen when we pass the world's edge?" 948D-21 queried. "Shall we keep on going straight or turn with the contour of the planet?"

"We shall turn—of that I am sure," said the professor. "But at what level we shall continue to cruise above the surface is problematical. The gravity in the two end zones of this great slab is much greater than the attraction of any of the other four facets. It also presents the least amount of surface, although that consists of territory enclosed by four thousand miles on one side and fourteen thousand miles on the other. We have never landed on this end, although we paid a brief visit to the other end; from end to end there is a diameter of twenty-three thousand miles. We shall certainly be drawn closer to the surface than we are now."

Appraised of what was to happen, the music monsters were all eyes and interest. Little had they known of the world on which they lived, and what they now saw they scarcely understood. In musical conversation, they remarked on the weirdness of it all, this strangest of all adventures.

The spaceship kept on past the planet fragment, as if it were destined to float off into space away from the mighty slab, yet expectantly the machine men waited for the right angle shift which they knew would come. They were beyond the cross view of the atmosphere, in a position where they were able to view slantingly the end country of the planet fragment, before the professor noticed any change in their course. There was no right-angle turn such as a vehicle or traveler might have executed on the surface. The initial perception consisted of the illusion that the spaceship had dropped more on a level with the lengthwise facet it was leaving, yet was still continuing away from the strangely formed world. The spaceship slowly described a curve which brought it into the darkened end territory of the irregular mass and settled into the darkness closer to the ground.

V

SUNLIGHT FADED out of view beyond the world's rim they were leaving behind. In impenetrable darkness, except for the stars above them, they coursed above this unexplored territory. Below them, all lay black.

"At our present rate of speed, how long will it take us to pass this end of the world?" asked 454ZQ2.

"For some reason or other, our speed of drift has slowed down, and we are settling closer to the surface," 29G-75 informed them.

"I expected the latter to occur," said the professor, "but why should our speed abate?"

"Something about the nature of the unmanageable controls. They have become affected by the greater gravity in this end zone."

"We may fall," suggested 948D-21 cryptically.

"We have the gauges to watch. We can only wait and see what happens."

"Are they reliable?"

"They seem to have remained undamaged."

All through the darkness, the machine men kept vigil over the gauges, watching the alarming tendency of the uncontrolled ship to slip over planet-ward. Uncertain of the gauges in the darkness where they could see nothing, the machine men occasionally tested space outside to discern possible traces of atmosphere, to see if they were closer to the ground than the gauges showed them to be. Already the gauges showed their position to be slightly more than an elevation of twenty miles, but here in the end territory, the atmosphere lay more compact and dense, the outer limits of the air having a lower altitude due to the intense gravitational attraction.

The machine men were relieved when a weak but growing dawn supplanted the night and they were able to see where they were. Below them lay a vast panorama of land and water, desert and vegetation, hills, mountains, valleys and plains. The mountains cut across one corner of the facet and were not so high as those seen by the machine men on other portions of the planet fragment. The music monsters were complaining of gnawing hunger, yet were still reluctant about eating their enemies, the fire-dwellers.

By the time the sun had arisen like a ball of incandescence out of the sea of air beyond the rim, the spaceship had dropped to the alarming altitude of only five miles. No longer were the machine men in doubt. The immense gravity of the planet fragment was drawing them down. What was more, their descent was sufficiently fast to threaten their safety when the spaceship landed.

"Get out the mechanical wings and the degravitators," the professor told them. "If we have to abandon ship on

142

the wing, the degravitators will be necessary. Experience down on the other end taught us that."

"What about the music monsters?"

"We may not have to abandon ship. It is only a possibility. If we do, we can wait until the last two miles and carry them with us."

"Is there nothing we can do to save the ship?"

"Nothing. We must trust to chance."

"It will be long before we can ever repair it and leave this world."

"It may be longer before the rest of our number discover our whereabouts," observed 29G-75 pessimistically. "For all they know, we might have drifted off in space. They will wait for us to return, not knowing that we cannot do so."

The mechanical wings and degravitators were donned, and the two music monsters were equipped with the degravitators and given their instructions. The machine men had considered the little space cars carried in the ship, but these were largely dependent on remote control from the ship, and here again the unmanageable condition of the ship's controls blocked them from an assured avenue of safety. The degravitators were like those the organic Zoromes used on the large planet Dompt of their own system and called gravity nullifiers.

Closer they fell toward the planet fragment, the machine men anxiously scanning the gauges, the music monsters excited and tense, fully cognizant of the dread circumstances they were facing. Within four miles of the surface above a vegetated plain, the professor noticed a lessening of their downward drop; he attributed it to the denser atmosphere near the ground. Still, the pace was one sufficiently dangerous to their welfare, especially to that of the music monsters.

With Arminia in his tentacles, the professor stood ready at the door of the spaceship prepared to leap. Behind him stood 948D-21 with the other music monster. 29G-75 and 454ZQ2 had elected to stay until the spaceship was nearly to the ground. At a mile and a half altitude, secure that the music monsters would suffer no harm at this low level, the professor and 948D-21 leaped out of the spaceship. Arminia gave vent to a melody of terror as the professor's mechanical wings failed of instant action and they plunged like a stone, whirling giddily. But the professor did not bring himself up sharp, for fear of the excessive gravity wrenching

Arminia from his grasp, and so he decreased their falling speed slowly while clinging tightly to his larger companion.

This one terrific plunge had sped the professor down ahead of the spaceship and 948D-21, and he landed to watch the falling bulk of the ship. With a musical sigh of relief, Arminia slumped to the ground, having been thoroughly scared out of his wits and never before in his life having ever felt so thankful. 948D-21 and his charge were still small objects in the sky beside the huge spaceship. The professor believed now that the ship's descent had slowed even more, yet he dared not feel positive, for his standing position below might have given him a deceptive perspective. 948D-21 was flying not far from the ship in concentrated spirals, waiting to land after the ship had struck.

Immovable, Professor Jameson watched fearfully as the ship neared the ground. The remaining machine men had not leaped. The professor watched for them. They did not appear. With a dull crash which the professor knew had sprung many plates and joints, the spaceship struck. 454ZQ2 and 29G-75 had elected to remain on board. Leaving Arminia to make his way as best he could, the professor hurried to the spaceship, which had plunged awkwardly into the ground and lay on one side. Dodging bushes and plants and frightening queer little animals from his path, the professor arrived at the side of the ship just as 948D-21 came to rest on the ground with the music monsters. Climbing out upon the hull came 454ZQ2 and 29G-75.

"It might have been worse," philosophized 29G-75. "The injuries to the ship are not wholly irreparable, but we can do nothing until the others arrive."

"Why did you stay aboard?"

"We saw that it would be comparatively safe to stay. After you leaped, the ship continued to slow down."

The machine men were aware of a shrill, despairing melody from where the professor had left Arminia. The other music monster was first to respond, and his haste to reach his distressed comrade met with ludicrious failure. Unprepared for the strange influence of the degravitators he wore, the music monster took two or three unstable movements and tumbled into a gyrating summersault, sprawling upon the ground.

In dumbfounded despair, Arminia was trying to walk toward them. He had divested himself of the gravity nullifiers and like a man with an overwhelming burden he was staggering toward them, his muscles bulging, his eyes

144

dilated and every lifting of his lower legs accompanied by a super-effort. His upper appendages hung limply at his sides, and his breathing came in laboring sobs.

Hurrying to where Arminia had left the gravity nullifiers, the professor retrieved them and replaced them on the ankles of the music monster. Instantly, Arminia's fatigue disappeared as if by magic, and the change was manifested no more surprisingly than in the expression on his face. In confused relief, he started forward once more, staggered, righted himself and then walked carefully toward the spaceship with the professor. Once the professor seized him as he was about to duplicate the previous gymnastic contortions of his companion by an attempt at quickening his pace.

"Not until you two are more acquainted with the degravitators," warned the professor. "It takes time and practice before you can become accustomed to walking with them, let alone running. You will take some bad spills unless you are careful. And if you value your lives, do not remove them as Arminia did just now."

The two music monsters were more deliberate in their movements from then on, and not even the prospects of alleviating their hunger caused them to forget the penalties of haste. Arminia was first to reach one of the plants which towered slightly about his head. Long, drooping leaves arched away from a peculiarly marked stalk whose top rounded into a purple-tinted ball. The general color of the vegetation was brown. Here and there, the younger growth was yellowish, while slate-colored stalks were not so numerous. Many of the stalks were gone, as if they had been removed by someone or something. Arminia was going to eat, and his companion, arriving behind him, prepared to assist in breaking off the seemingly delectable stalk from its base.

Whip-like tendrils wrapped themselves sinuously about the two music monsters and the leaves folded devilishly about them. They struggled fiercely, but the tough tendrils held like steel. Emitting a weird sympony of surprise, rage and fear, the two music montsers battled and tore at the plant: Arminia ripping and tearing at the tough, leathery stalk and leaves with his hook, his companion too pinioned to permit him to reach a weapon. Where the hook sank deep, there immediately issued a thick, purple liquid that coagulated almost instantly, leaving a shining, dull surface.

"Carnivorous plants!" 29G-75 exclaimed. "We have not seen such things for many a journey!"

Already, Professor Jameson was hurrying to the rescue

145

of the hopelessly entangled music monsters. He played his heat ray upon the base of the plant, knowing that as soon as it was cut from the ground it would weaken and die. The plant writhed and whipped its leaves frantically like a creature in pain, the tendrils constricting with such strength as to choke off the music monsters' weird cacophony and turn them blue in the face. And then came the unexpected. It surprised the machine men and left them strangely impressed. The plant screamed.

Its leaves in a frenzy of motion, an opening in the purple ball appeared, and from it there issued an indescribable scream, one of the most awesome sounds ever to fall upon the mechanical hearing of the machine men. If the fire-dwellers had proved difficult to kill with the heat ray, the case of these carnivorous plants proved quite the opposite. In a final frenzy, with a dying screech, which chilled the blood of its two prospective victims, the plant sagged and commenced to wilt, its tendrils releasing their grip and jerking spasmodically, falling to the ground bent away from the spot where the professor had applied his heat ray.

Shaken and unnerved, the two music monsters were speechless, for once without a song, while they got back their breath. It was the closest either of them had ever come to dying, although Arminia had thought the plunge from the sky the most horrible sensation he had ever experienced. The humor of the near tragedy became apparent to the professor.

"You came to eat them; they nearly ate you. They are of a vegetable character and prefer a diet of flesh and blood; you are flesh and blood and are strict vegetarians. What contrasts!"

"You can eat now," observed 29G-75.

"I am not hungry," said Arminia. "I seem to have lost my appetite."

The music monsters did, however, eat of the fallen plant later on, after more of the strange plants had been examined, and they found their repast both delectable and satisfying after their fast on the spaceship. Careful examination of the tall plants, which grew quite numerous over the plain, showed that many creatures had been captured and digested, their white bones strewn about the base of the plants. The carnivorous species of vegetation did not, however, seem to find such an animal diet necessary, for those not fortunate enough to have captured an animal seemed healthy and luxuriant. Partly digested remains of a small animal gripped by one of the plants illustrated how the victims were digested. A sticky juice was exuded from the tendrils which enwrapped the repast securely.

Again, the machine men noticed the different stages in color and growth. The small, young ones were yellow. Most of the mature plants were brownish in color, with the purple top strangely suggestive of a head. Older and more advanced. What they did find difficult to explain were the dead, abandoned plants without stalks.

"Some creature around here is more powerful than these plants and robs them of their stalks," observed 29G-75 reflectively. "It is a good thing to know. We shall have to be on the watch for them."

"The plants themselves possess tremendous strength," Arminia reminded them.

"Anything here that could live under these conditions would have to be strong," said 948D-21, "just as the Ooaurs were so much stronger than the Uum."

"There is one piece of evidence that stands against the plants being subdued by force," the professor stated. "The leaves are intact, showing that there could have been no struggle. It is possible that the stalks are removed after the plant dies."

The machine men made another startling discovery as they wandered among the placid-appearing plants waiting so silently and quietly for victims. They recognized familiar shapes, globular and possessing many small tentacles, entangled in the twines of the carnivorous plants. They were Eiuks.

"Evidently they are capable of living here, too," the professor observed. "Their remarkable qualities of becoming living balloons during the day make them resistant even to the gravity here."

In examination of the various exhibits consisting of the living plants and their dead victims, 454ZQ2 stepped too close to the plant they were examining, brushing the long arched leaves with his tentacles. Instantly he was seized and gathered to the deadly embrace of the vicious plant, the tendrils playing, writhing and clutching over him in joyous ecstasy. The professor leaped forward with his heat ray, yet hesitated to see what 454ZQ2 might be able to do, realizing that here was no danger such as had menaced the music monsters. The strength of the plant was amazing, yet here in this plant there was no hard exterior such as had characterized the fire-dwellers. The metal tentacles bit into

147

the tendrils until the machine man was empurpled with the plant's fluid. Jerking and flailing his tentacles, 454ZQ2 ripped the leaves into ribbons and belabored the plant to a purple welter with kicking feet and lashing tentacles.

The two music monsters were amazed and impressed by this demonstration. They had been helpless in the embrace of the plant which had captured them. The machine man had effected an easy victory. On the other hand, the fire-dwellers had proved to be more of a problem to the Zoromes than to the music monsters, although at no time except in the fire country were the machine men actually endangered in physical combat.

The machine men and music monsters spent the night in the spaceship. They had not yet decided what was to be done. During the night, strange noises were occasionally heard outside, yet none of them investigated beyond peering out of the spaceship. 454ZQ2 once saw dim forms flit out of range of his body lights. Pursuit was considered inadvisable under their present circumstances.

In the morning, several discoveries were made. For one thing, strange tracks were found, and another closely linking feature was the absence of several stalks from the carnivorous plants which were of the aged variety. Tracks surrounded the old plants. Evidently creatures of some kind had come in the night and had carried off several of the stalks. His curiosity aroused, the professor claimed that the next time the nocturnal sounds were heard they would turn out with the ray guns and surprise the marauders. One strange circumstance seemed especially inexplicable. One set of tracks led to a missing stalk and then disappeared. Whether the creature had been coming or going was difficult to ascertain from the strange pattern left by the feet, but there was only one set of them, and the thing, whatever it was that had robbed the plant of its stalk, had traveled in but one direction. The suggestion of 29G-75 was the most plausible.

"Whatever they are, they have wings, or else they are able to rise like the Eiuks."

"It was certainly not the Eiuks, for they are preyed upon by the plants."

"Perhaps," offered 948D-21, "the old plants are unable to resist the Eiuks who rise up with the stalks."

"It is improbable, for we should have seen the shining globes of the Eiuks had they come last night," stated the professor. "Besides, the Eiuks do not leave tracks like those we saw, assuming that those who took the stalks made the tracks."

Taking council, the four Zoromes decided that on the following day two of them, 454ZQ2 and 29G-75, would don the mechanical wings and the degravitators and would head back upon the long journey to the fire country upon another side of the planet fragment. Professor Jameson estimated their position as roughly sixteen thousand miles from the land of the music monsters.

"How will 744U-21, 20R-654 and the others, necessary for the repair of the spaceship, be able to get back here?" 454ZQ2 posed the ultimate consideration.

"You can carry extra mechanical wings and gravity nullifiers," the professor instructed them. "Of course, the degravitators will be necessary only above this end of the fragment. Instead of crossing the three thousand miles of this country directly to the thicker side of the fragment, it is more advisable to go directly to the thin facet which is less than fifteen hundred miles distant and then cut diagonally over upon the thicker side of the planet. You will experience easier going and the difference in the distance will be more or less negligible."

Again that night the strange noises were heard, this time at a greater distance, and, being prepared, the four machine men hurried out cautiously into the dark. The music monsters remained behind in the ship. For one thing, the latter possessed little stomach for the unknown terrors of this strange land, and they had to be careful about walking with the gravity nullifiers. Then, too, the professor considered it inadvisable for them to hazard running against one of the sinister plants in the dark. These plants were man-eaters, had the music monsters been men instead of what they were.

VI

THE MACHINE MEN did not find it necessary to risk appraising the nocturnal unknowns of their presence with use of their body lights. A strange glow which the machine men readily recognized pervaded the landscape, casting a dim, ghastly radiance upon the weird scene beneath the starlight.

The Eiuks had dropped from the sky. There were at least a hundred of them, the professor estimated, and immediately he gathered the significance of so many more of them than he had ever seen descend upon Ui. The greater gravity was sufficient to pull down many of them involuntarily when their gaseous propensities were at the lowest ebb. The machine men had never known whether the Eiuks descended voluntarily or not. Like the carnivorous plants, the Eiuks did not seem dependent on flesh and blood for sustenance, but they seemed particularly ravenous for it, when the opportunity offered. In that particular, Professor Jameson likened them to the leech and mosquito of his much earlier life.

Already, several of the shining globes had met the misfortune of falling into the eager clutches of the tall plants, and they represented a weird appearance as the tendrils and leaves embraced their brilliance, tinting the ground about them with a purple glow as if shades of the same color had been drawn upon the brilliance of the Eiuks. The latter presented a weak resistance, and soon their bright glow waned as death claimed them and the plants eagerly sapped and drained their vitality into the tendrils and leaves.

To this the machine men paid but scant, secondary consideration. The ghostlike, flitting forms among the vegetation riveted their attention. Ominous and of sinister, evil portent, they scampered excitedly among the falling globes. Each one seized an Eiuk and started off for the distant hills, bouncing away as the alarmed denizens of the upper air tried to break free. Instinctively, aware of their peril, the rest of the shining globes rose and bounced about, trying to escape the clutches of the snatching, leaping creatures. Between them and the horrid, waiting embrace of the plants, the Eiuks were hard set, but now they were becoming more difficult to capture.

Creeping closer, unobserved, the four Zoromes watched the deadly contest and were impressed by a strange coincidence of the carnivorous plants and the creatures from the hills both intent on capturing the Eiuks. When one of the slinking creatures seized an Eiuk, there came the flash of purple light shining through the clutching arms, similar to its manner of glowing through the leaves and tendrils of the plants. The machine men wondered why the plants did not catch these other marauders as well as the Eiuks, yet they had previously figured that it was these same marauders who had carried off the stalks from the plants.

There was much to be understood, and to understand it better, the machine men walked closer to the scene of the chase, stepping into the aura of pale radiance hanging

150

about the vicinity of the Eiuks like a transparent fog. They were immediately seen by several roving hunters who had not yet made their captures. The rest were in a long line of the things scampering off toward the hills, each lighted by a living torch held high, so that their path of retreat became marked by a bobbing, serpentine column of gradually dwindling globes of light. Before the machine men could fairly have their ray ejectors ready for the inevitable, the unburdened things charged down upon them viciously. Most of them fell before the blazing death which swept into their vitals, but a few reached the machine men unscathed and wrestled with them.

Cold, curling tentacles, snakelike, wound about the four Zoromes and roved feelingly over their metal heads and bodies, showing surprising strength and tenacity in their grip as they sought to drag down the machine men and choke and smother them—at least, such was the professor's fleeting impression. If this was the expectation of the strange things, the anticipation became rudely shattered.

It was all over so soon, it had happened so rapidly, that the machine men were surprised to find themselves standing alone among the scattered dead upon whom shone the ghastly, funereal radiance of the bobbing Eiuks. The machine men had their first opportunity for a close examination of the evil-intentioned things they had previously seen only as indistinct shadows.

Professor Jameson was met with one of the greatest surprises of his entire career among the machine men of Zor. The dead forms scattered over the ground, fallen before the terrible heat rays and in actual combat with the Zoromes, were the missing stalks from the carnivorous plants! They had been alive, sentient and capable of locomotion! Here was the reply to the question of the missing stalks. For several moments, the machine men were too stunned with this electrifying discovery to reason out the solution.

"Are they plant or animal?"

"Both."

"No—they are animal now; they were once plants."

"They grew as plants—"

"And became animals at the proper time of evolution."

The lower half of the stalks branched off into four legs possessing tiny, round feet. When drawn together, they appeared as a solid pillar. The machine men recollected striated lines running the length of the stalks, but they had attached no peculiar significance to them, partly hidden as they were by the broad, arching leaves. Now they knew why the plants had screamed. It had been surprising that the plant-animals had made no outcry during the recent fray, yet the machine men had burnt them down and throttled them so quickly that their silence had been more or less enforced. They noticed something else now that they had not seen before: the purple head possessed several small knobs which the machine men identified as optics. The purple liquid, the life-blood of the things, had impressed them from the first with its thick qualities so divergent from usual plant life. But they had catalogued it merely as a characteristic peculiar to this type of plant. The machine men now wondered if the plants were watching with their beady eyes. The tall stalks had taken on a new and ominous significance.

The next morning, 29G-75 and 454ZQ2 equipped themselves and set out upon their long journey. Both 948D-21 and the professor would have liked to have gone, too, but it was their duty to stay by the ship. Had this necessity not existed, there would have been a problem presented by the two music monsters. The latter were told the strange story of the missing stalks, and how the long tendrils of the plant were really living tentacles. It would be long before the machine men would reach the edge of the fire country and as long again before they returned with companions. What if 744U-21 and the rest of the Zoromes should not be there when 29G-75 and 454ZQ2 terminated their long journey? Professor Jameson had reason to believe that the machine men would stay where they were in the land of the music monsters. At the very least, they would establish a base of communication for the lost ship and its occupants. Many possibilities presented themselves, yet the two waiting machine men realized that their adopted course was the only present solution. They hoped that 29G-75 and 454ZQ2 would reach the edge of the fire country without mishap.

They had much time during their enforced wait to observe the carnivorous plants in their various stages of evolution. Occasionally, one of them in company with the music monsters roamed far afield, penetrating to the hills where the plant-animals lived in packs within the dense brush country. It was in the lowlands, where the ship had fallen, that the plant-animals became developed. At an early phase of their development, seeds and pollen were scattered to the winds. One plant never grew more than a single stalk, and when the stalk became sufficiently developed to leave its vegetable state of existence, it disengaged its feet, gradually separated from the rest of the plant and left under cover of darkness, abandoning the plant as if it were an old chrysalis.

Whether the plants possessed eyesight during the vegetable stage, the professor was unable to accurately ascertain, but he came to believe that the older ones did when he had employed the simple experiment of holding up one of the music monsters close to the purple head of a maturing plant. The fixed eyes became animated with a subtle gleam from their baleful depths, and without the usual necessity of contact the tendrils commenced to quiver excitedly and reach out for the delectable morsel. Sometimes, one of the machine men would fly alone farther than it was possible to go in company with the music monsters. Beyond the hills lay another low plain where the carnivorous plants grew both profusely and luxuriantly. Beyond the plain rose the mountains. It was in these mountains that the Eiuks resided, the machine men believed.

There were other species of animal besides the plant-things and the Eiuks, but mostly they were smaller, inferior creatures. A close, short verdure grew all over the plain, which also supported other forms of plant life, much in minority to the carnivorous species, which seemed to dominate and absorb nutrition from the ground. In the hill country, thick with bushes and other types of vegetation, there were none of these hideous plants.

Professor Jameson advanced a theory, dealing with the tremendous gravity of the end territory, that explained tentatively this strange phenomenon of the hybrid plant-animal species they had discovered.

"Life is a determined factor and cleverly surmounts almost insuperable obstacles, becoming readily adaptable to the environment in which it finds itself. Consider the fire-dwellers, for example. Their situation is no less astounding and miraculous than what we find here. A strong type of life is required in this end zone. Some of the creatures here have developed without the vegetable beginning, yet there is a peculiarity of the plant-animals, one which necessitates their start in life strictly as a plant. When young, they must be very weak and unable to start life in mobile form. The plant-animals developed like the rest of the various forms of life from a simple cellular structure, becoming first a plant

153

and then an animal. In the early, weaker stages, the necessity of locomotion for seeking sustenance is done away with by their remaining in one spot and drawing life from the soil. They are also carnivorous. I believe we shall find that in their strictly animal stages they are entirely carnivorous."

Arminia, more venturesome than his companion, was not satisfied until he had killed one of the plant-animals in combat and brought the carcass back to the spaceship, incidentally winning a bet his comrade had made on the assumption that he could not do it and would have to fall back upon the help of the machine men. The two music monsters had skinned their late enemies and cured the hides. They had derived much amusement in throwing chunks from the carcasses of the fire-dwellers to the carnivorous plants. Deprived of their dice and metallic squares, the two had gambled lavishly in all sorts of imaginative forms, even as to guessing the exact time the horizon would cut the rising sun in half, using instruments of the Zoromes for reckoning the time. Their funds were practically unlimited, since they had redeemed the pelts of their erstwhile enemies, and they gambled to their hearts' content, fortune and prosperity smiling first on one and then on the other.

After their first clash with the machine men, the separated stalks kept away from the vicinity of the spaceship, staying in their hill country. The night following the killing of so many of the plant-things, they had returned and found the carcasses of the brethren. When the sun rose again, the dead were gone.

Time passed, and sunset followed sunset. The music monsters commenced to fail in health from the tremendous attraction of gravity, despite the degravitators they always wore and those they kept installed in their living quarters. It was still much too early to expect the return of the machine men. When they came, the professor intended that Arminia and his companion be carried on the wing to the not so distant area of lowest gravity. They would recover rapidly there, for the resistance would be even less than in their own country, which represented the antipode of the facet on which dwelled the Ooaurs.

So the machine men were completely surprised when ahead of schedule some very small blots appeared in the sky. The blots materialized into two varieties, flying machine men and round globes.

"The Oaos!" 948D-21 exclaimed. "How did they happen to come?"

His question remained unanswered until eight machine men flew down from the sky, leaving the metal Oaos on high. It was 744U-21 and 6W-438 who explained matters.

"When 29G-75 and 454ZQ2 returned on the wing without the spaceship and told us where you had fallen, we knew that a long and arduous task lay before us of getting ourselves and the necessities for repair of the ship here into this isolated end territory, facing the handicap of such immense gravity. So we sent a winged courier down over the other side of the planet fragment to the land of the Urum for their aid."

"What it would have taken us an exceedingly long time to accomplish they can expedite. We are all here, 21M-M392; that is, the remainder are at the world's edge bordering what the Urum would probably call the Land of Greatest Exhaustion."

"Why did they not come, too?" 948D-12 asked.

"Most of us were brought here to the edge of the end zone in the aircraft of the Urum, accompanied by the Oaos. Eight of us came on the wing equipped with the degravitators which you sent to us by 454ZQ2 and 29G-75. The Oaos came with us, directed by remote control from the airships of the Urum. The Urum dare not bring their airships into this end zone or come themselves. The Oaos, of course, operate on gaseous principles analogous to the aerial faculties of the Eiuks. The Urum and the rest of the machine men are waiting at the world's edge."

Soon, all the machine men were about the wrecked spaceship with the necessary material and facilities brought from Uri for its repairs. 29G-75 and 454ZQ2 had taken back with them exact, detailed accounts of the damage done the spaceship, both inside and out. The damage was greatest to the hull and compartments nearest the point where the ship had struck the ground.

Many long days and nights of intensive, untiring work were necessary. Often, the machine men were surrounded at night not only by their own illumination, but by the light of the Eiuks as well, presenting a weird scene. The animated plant stalks gazed fearfully down from the distant hills, as near as they dared approach the mixture of natural and unnatural brilliance. The first trip back to the base, situated at the world's rim bordering the flat world of least gravity and the end zone, had seen the departure of the two ailing music monsters—singing their duo of melancholia. At the base, they had found many of their companions, who had accompanied the Urum and machine men in the airships. The recovery of the two music monsters was rapid as they joined their companions in jumping and skipping in gigantic leaps much like those of the Ooaurs by the walls of Ui.

Immensely rich in the square bits of fire-dweller hide which the two music monsters had insisted in bringing out of the end zone—and thus loading down a single machine man with them and with nothing else—the music monsters made gifts among their companions and gambled so recklessly and rapidly that the fever spread to the curious and interested Disci of Uri. Long geared music monsters squatted incongruously with the diminutive Disc creatures and passed much time in gaming, the latter much impressed with admiration and wonderment at the musical innuendoes of their new friends, whom they understood only in pantomime or through the able interpretation of the Zoromes. Much to the delight of Arminia and his companion so long "imprisoned" by the necessity of wearing gravity nullifiers, their companions had brought the many pictured dice and square bits of metal.

Only once did several of the Urum, much laden with gravity nullifiers, venture into the end zone in company with similarly equipped music monsters and machine men to witness the amazing phenomena of the carnivorous plants and watch a nocturnal disengagement of a ripe stalk. The sight of the gently falling Eiuks was familiar to the Urum, though never before had they seen so many of them descend at one time. A strange sense of satisfaction enveloped them as they saw the carnivorous plants make their catches of the Eiuks who came too close. Too often had the Disci fled into their homes in terror from the nocturnal raids of the shining balls.

When the spaceship was at last capable of flight once more, the entire assemblage was taken for a trip low above the end territory of the planet fragment before once again revisiting the land of the Urum and then back to the forests bordering the fire country. With the various functions of the ship once more intact, the gravity of the end zone remained a negligible factor.

The machine men and music monsters lingered in the land of the Urum for some time, beside the gaunt, towering mountains which stretched their fingers into space, before returning to the forest retreats of the music monsters upon the facet opposite the Land of Exhausion. Here, they renewed their visit so abruptly interrupted by the unexpected raid of the fire-dwellers.

Finally there came the irresistible call of unseen worlds, the lure of the universe. With the farewell melody of the music monsters behind them and the silent star symphony before, the machine men departed from the huge, rugged, misshapen world on which they had encountered so many strange adventures among stranger forms of life. Behind them dwindled the glowing oval of soft, steady light which marked the retreating planet fragment; ahead, many light years beyond the system of worlds they were leaving, stretched a dense, black pocket of emptiness where no stars shone.

DON'T MISS THESE GREAT ADVENTURES
IN TIME-TRAVEL INTRIGUE!

G-605   AGENT OF T.E.R.R.A. #1:
The Flying Saucer Gambit by Larry Maddock

Hannibal Fortune and his symbiotic partner Webley come to Earth to investigate the murder of T.E.R.R.A.'s Resident Agent in the 20th Century.

G-620   AGENT OF T.E.R.R.A. #2:
The Golden Goddess Gambit by Larry Maddock

Fortune and Webley fight a desperate battle against time-tampering by EMPIRE agents in the dawn of Earth's history.

G-644   AGENT OF T.E.R.R.A. #3:
The Emerald Elephant Gambit by Larry Maddock

Fortune and Webley must battle to insure the destruction of a great civilization, while vicious looters from the far future upset the balance of history.

CLASSICS OF GREAT SCIENCE-FICTION

from ACE BOOKS